MW00965340

# 2 0 2 0
## Vol. 4

| | |
|---|---|
| EDITOR IN CHIEF | Laura Kepner |
| MANAGING EDITOR | Warren Firschein |
| ART DIRECTOR | Carrie Font Granato |
| POETRY EDITORS | Nancy Bruckner |
| | Barbara Finkelstein |
| | D. Klein |
| PROSE EDITORS | Amy Bryant |
| | Warren Firschein |
| | Carrie Font Granato |
| ASSOCIATE EDITOR | Sophie Goldsmith |

Published jointly by

SAFETY HARBOR WRITERS & POETS
CHAPTER TWO PRESS

This is the final volume of *Odet*, which was published annually from 2017-2020. Contact us at OdetJournal@gmail.com, or by mail at Odet Journal, c/o Chapter Two Press, P.O. Box 870, Safety Harbor, FL 34695. To order copies of any of our four volumes, visit www.chaptertwopress.com.

Printed in the United States of America
Cover art by George Chase
Cover design by Carrie Font Granato
The text type was set in Plantin

*Dedicated to all the writers, poets, and artists*

*who have been a part of our journey.*

VOLUME FOUR • 2020

# Odet

## PHOTOGRAPHERS AND ARTISTS

Additional uncredited artwork throughout this volume by Shelly Miller

### 2019 ROMEO LEMAY WRITING CONTEST

    ★       First Prize Winners
  ★★       Second Prize Winners

### 2019 ROGER HOWARD POETRY PRIZE

    †       First Prize Winner
  ††      Second Prize Winner
 †††     Honorable Mention

# To Our Readers:

Welcome to the fourth (and largest!) volume of *Odet*, an annual journal for Florida-based writers, poets, and artists. As in the past, we're thrilled to award prizes through the annual Romeo Lemay contest, generously funded by Romeo's son Tim and administered by *Safety Harbor Writers & Poets*. All winning entries are included in this journal and are indicated in the table of contents. Romeo wrote of his experiences growing up near Quebec during the Depression, and we are pleased to present one of his essays, "The Last Train Out," which fits our annual theme.

For the first time, we have offered a separate prize for poets, named after Roger Howard and funded by his wife. Roger, a previous contributor to *Odet*, was a local writer who became a poet late in life after he had finished a career as a surgeon. We have included one of his poems, "Black Lined Roads," for your enjoyment.

The theme for this edition is "Point A to Point B," which refers not only to physical journeys, but internal ones as well. At *Odet*, we began our own journey in 2016, when, armed with only enthusiasm and faith, we took our first steps. Representative of our growth, we are proud to report that this past summer we finished second in the voting for the best literary journal produced in the Tampa Bay region. We can't thank enough those writers, poets, and artists who believed in us and stuck with us over the years despite our growing pains and frequent missteps.

But every journey must reach an end, and this is ours. We are saddened to announce that, due to recent changes in our personal lives that would hamper future efforts, this will be the final volume of *Odet*. In reflecting on this difficult decision, we recognize how much we have grown professionally through *Odet*—as well as the numerous friends we've made. Several of you have contributed to each of the four volumes, a true achievement, and we humbly salute you. We'd like to specifically thank those individuals who have been a part of this journal through the years, helping through the selection, editing, illustrating, and formatting processes. This includes, in alphabetical order, Nancy Bruckner, Amy Bryant, Nicole Caron, Barbara Finkelstein, Sophie Goldsmith, Carrie Granato, Ari Kepner, Deb Klein, and Chris Shaun. These talented folks were always willing to offer their expertise, energy, and (most of all) their time, and without their assistance, *Odet* would have forever remained just a theoretical topic for discussion at polite (and not-so-polite) cocktail parties.

While this is the end of *Odet*, we certainly expect it isn't the end of our contributors' artistic output. We can't wait to read your future work and hear of your success. See you around.

Warren Firschein & Laura Kepner

# Abuelo and the Lector

When Joaquina was a girl, her abuelo told her
*You're sweet as the best tobacco leaf.*
These days, in the nursing home, he doesn't
recognize her, but his fingertips roll
from their own memory, invisible cigars.

Some days he rolls perfectas, fat and prime,
other days, cherutos, smaller, quicker.
Cut and roll, cut and roll, the young tabaquero
rolls 125 a day. These days his hands flap like wings
unless he's weighing imaginary leaves in his palms.

When Joaquina speaks, her abuelo hears only
El Lector en la tribuna, reading high above
the work tables. A thinking man who doesn't
remember he's forgotten how to think, he awaits
daily readings from adventurous times, places never seen.

He wonders if Cuba will soon be free from Spain,
requests Cervantes, Tolstoy, Jules Verne.
Joaquina reads clearly, her abuelo tapping on the table
a tabaquero's admiration. His rolling hand pauses briefly,

retrieves a quarter from his pocket to pay the lector
his portion of the weekly wage. Joaquina places
a paper ring on his finger. When she goes home her abuelo's
hands stop still, on strike until the manufacturers agree
to let the lector return to the imaginary factory.

The next day, upon her arrival, his hands
once again remember the 75 movements needed
for one simple cigar. Cut and roll, cut and roll,
his history she can no longer see, yet can almost
smell like a magic veil over Ybor City.

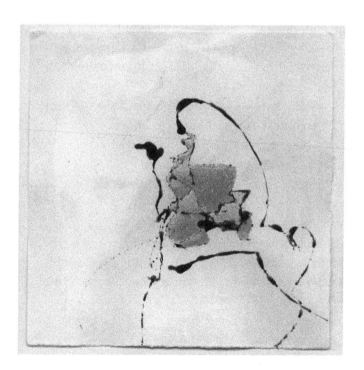

# Looking Up

She stood by the entrance to the lighthouse, holding colorful dollar store gloves. I was surprised to see her but then I had no inkling of the moment's significance. Do we ever? I thought I was there to cheer on a local hero, a woman who a year ago was paralyzed but was today going to ascend the 219 winding iron steps of the local lighthouse. Not something I would ever do, but I'm no superhero.

My spidey senses should have been tingling madly; that dark circular staircase was a wrought iron metaphor for my own twisty climb back from the brink. But it was really only in the past year or so that I had acknowledged the road, let alone recognized the movement of my spirit. How is that even possible? I think of those moving walkways used in airports, transporting us as we passively stare straight ahead. It's possible to move through your own life in a similar fashion, feeling almost submerged, the sounds muted and fuzzy.

The first four years after losing my son were very much a case of putting one foot in front of the other. I don't know any other way to get through that kind of pain. There is no reasonable expectation; reason left the building that summer morning along with my sweet Zachary. But at the same time, I knew enough to keep moving. Movement was key. To stay in that place of stunned brokenness was unfathomable. So I kept walking, a wounded, limping deer in the headlights of a grief train barreling down the tracks. Each step a victory, a refusal to lie down.

Not that I didn't laugh along the way and eat fine food, do laundry, and take vacations. I did all of those things and even enjoyed some of them. But it wasn't fully me. It was someone who looked like me, answered to my name. But she was off in some significant ways. Not fully present. My crazy showed itself in a variety of manifestations, some pitiful, some actually funny. I can laugh now at the two years spent insisting I was in my forties when really I was in my sixties. No idea why. Was I trying to turn back time? The brain has its own way of functioning, completely apart from our control or wisdom.

That's really a big part of what it's about, isn't it? That loss of control. Who knew you could walk downstairs one morning and find the world had turned utterly inside out and upside down? It's amazing how even as years pass there's a small part of your brain . . . your heart, that still sometimes wonders for a few seconds upon waking . . . did that really happen?

My husband and I were relatively new to Florida, where we'd moved to expand our art business. So we were driving all over the state each weekend, setting up our tent and art in lovely towns, in beautiful parks and on breathtaking waterfronts. All we had to do was look up. The skies were the prettiest I'd ever seen, full of pink birds, snowy egrets, and lush greens. Sunshine sparkled brilliantly on water everywhere it seemed, reminding me that possibilities still existed. Our house sits across a meadow from an alligator farm, a local attraction that also is home to an estuary. So each new morning and closing dusk dazzling birds fly in and out, over my small yard, where I'd sit and drink in the hope, the healing. If your heart is broken, first thing to do? Move to Florida. Let the state do its wondrous thing on your spirit; you don't have to lift a finger. Just an eyelid, to let in the beauty. Turn the news off, go outside, and breathe. Let those pink roseate spoonbills do the heavy lifting in your soul.

About a year and a half ago I began to breathe easier, felt myself coming back closer to whom I used to be. I developed a deep thirst for books, spiritual books that spoke of positivity and hope, of redemption. I was reading everything I could get my hands on, and repeatedly getting the same message: give back. The road back is paved with intentional kindness, thoughtful giving. Moving away from self-focus and onto the needs of others. I tried a number of places, served several holiday dinners, before finding the spot that fit me best. Pie in the Sky collects, packs, and delivers groceries to seniors in need, and there I found my tribe. It's been several months now of twice-weekly packing sessions and I just took on my first regular delivery route this past week. I can't say enough about how good it feels to forget about me, to put the needs of others first for a change.

But my story is about more than that. The woman who started the program several years ago is a bit of a community fixture. Everyone knows Malea and the good she's done, not just for our seniors but also for the migrant farm workers barely surviving on the outskirts of town while picking the fruit and vegetables that fill our tables so bountifully each day. So when she woke up one morning with what was eventually diagnosed as Guillain-Barre syndrome, it was a shock to many of us. I followed her recovery on Facebook, watched her brutal struggle on the parallel bars, willing her feet to move again. When they announced at Pie one morning that Malea was climbing the local lighthouse in commemoration of the past year's fight to come back, I knew I wanted to be present to cheer her on. From the ground. Both feet planted solidly on terra firma.

And that's exactly what I told Tina when I saw her standing in front of the entrance that morning. My good friend explained that the gloves were for gripping the railing during the climb and tried to hand me a pair. Not necessary, I explained; my fear of heights was longstanding and well documented. Of course she said the usual things about not looking down and focusing only on the step in front of me, but all I heard was Charlie Brown's mother. *Wha wha wha.* I knew she meant well, but come on. A narrow circular staircase with steps you could see through? Not gonna happen.

And that was the position I took, right up until the moment I saw Malea. Inspiring does not even begin to cover it. Serving the poor *and* climbing the lighthouse steps a year after being paralyzed?! What a showoff. I slipped the gloves on with much fear and trembling and took my spot right behind her on the damn staircase. Glaring into her back as we climbed, me clinging to that railing, I half-hoped she could feel my rage rays beaming upon her spine. She stopped to rest on the landings, and I got to hear a bit more of her story, as her daughters and a local newscaster were climbing also, filming the exhilarating event. After a while I forgot to be a brat and began to realize not only what an honor it was to be there, but what an unexpected release it was becoming for me. We made our way past each of the 8 landings, all 219 steps, and when Malea came through the door on the top of the lighthouse I was right behind her, both of us grinning ear to ear.

I know this because I saw it on the news that night. Sure, the story was about Malea's triumph, as it should be. I like that my side tale is on the down low, known only to me. Only I know that stepping out onto that deck at the top was pushing back against the insecurities that had been trying to strangle me, to shut me down after the horrors of that morning when suddenly nothing seemed secure anymore. And there's truth in there; what is really secure in this world in the sense that it's never going to change? I needed to let that go. I needed to see again the beauty even in the precariousness of the climb.

This morning I was at the lighthouse again, making my way up those eight landings out onto the bright red deck. I go several times a week now, climbing three or four times at each visit. It's a great workout, and I've become friendly with several of the other regular climbers. But the benefits of this have gone way past the physical. It is more of a spiritual practice for me at this point. I gaze out over the sun glistening on the nearby ocean and the intercoastal, I watch the dolphins cavort and the palms sway in the breezes. And I remember that I have this day in which to be alive, to give back. I have this exhilarating gift of nature and beauty. If I forget, I can just watch that news clip again, and remember how much life likes to surprise us.

This morning I passed a couple on the lower landings as I made my way to the top, but on my way back down I found the woman sitting by herself about halfway up. I asked her if she'd changed her mind but I already suspected her answer. Sure enough, she said her fears had stopped her. I told her the briefest of summaries about my own first time, and how empowering it has become to me, how life changing. She was willing to give it another try, and together we made our way up the next four landings. Her husband's face when she stepped out onto the deck said it all and I quietly made my way around to the other side. Leaning into the sunbaked wall I gazed over the trees and water, all the way to the downtown sights, the red-roofed college buildings and the gleaming white sails of the tall ship docked in the harbor. I thought about those twisty iron steps that had brought me to all this beauty, all this wonder, and how well it reflects my own journey with its sorrows and its graces. Tomorrow is not promised, but look at all I have today, in this moment! Slipping my gloves back on, I blew a quick kiss toward the heavens for Zachary and started my descent, one grateful step at a time.

*Flowers*, Patrick Patterson

# Footprints

Impressed in red volcanic ash,
they are much like those I leave
on wet beach sand.
My lineage from the ones
who walked three million years ago,
leaving footprints behind,
cannot be denied.

Our relationship seems closer
than my kinship to great-grandparents
whom I have never known.
These ancient people,
who had no thought of me
or my time, have written a letter
on a page of Earth.

They were so small
in a world so large and alarming,
but they carried a spark to send them forth.
I have read their footprints,
imagining the continued trek that walked
their descendants beyond Africa,
to populate the entire planet.

Our family progressed
to speech and complex thought,
coming to believe that we are human
as those ancestors were not
and clinging to this belief
so we can claim the right
to stride like gods.

# Butterfly Shells

On our first cruise, you told me to walk along beaches carefully. *Watch the sand, not the waves,* you urged. You'd never say it with fear or warning. It was always with fascination.

The beaches along the lakes back home were muddy and littered with beer bottle tops, cigarette butts, and the dying coals of campsite fires. But on these beaches, sand covered your feet in a light dusting that then played with sunlight as it reflected off the hairs on your toes. At seven years old, on that first cruise, I was more fascinated by the aquamarine waves than the light display.

Years later, on the cruise we took just after you were told the cancer was back, I listened to your words and watched the sand.

We walked the beach nearest the port in Miami. You and I had two bags each: one for trash and one for whatever interested us as we moved down the coastline. You hummed a hymn I didn't know while I picked up broken shells that seagulls and tourists had ruined. You didn't bother to grab them, even when they had pretty swirls of purple on the underside or the shades of a sunset arching over their surface. Your bag for trash was full much quicker than mine was, your older eyes still keen enough to pick out tan cigarette butts from tan sand and bottle caps from seaweed, but my bag of treasures overflowed and you let me slip some into yours.

When I found a conch shell only missing its top spiral, I thought it was the best find of the day. Telling you I would take some leather cord and wrap the top to make a necklace filled the silence between us as we walked back to the bar that my parents had stopped at for drinks. You seemed like you were paying attention, but you were still scanning the beach.

Just before we turned from the waterline to head up toward the road, you stopped and squatted, taking three fingers to delicately urge something out of the sand. A near-white clam shell emerged, still connected at the center but split at the seams. You smiled to yourself, a smile that crinkled the corners of your eyes. *Found one,* you whispered, proudly. You didn't drop it in the bag, and instead bent your elbow, held your hand out with your palm facing the sand, the shell out so the two halves laid flat on your hand.

I asked *are those your favorite?* And you nodded, no verbal answer given as we climbed the concrete steps up to the sidewalk. The bar was across the street and my parents were outside, Dad's balding head already shining with a sunburn from our first day. They got up from the couch, Mom asking to see what I had brought back. Dad hugged you from the side so as not to jostle the hand you held out with the clam shell. He did it intentionally, unquizzically. Together we walked back to the hotel, a tired quiet encompassing us. We were ready to crawl into bed before boarding the ship the next day.

In the hotel room, I asked Mom and Dad about the way you carried the shell. You were back in your room, probably watching *Jeopardy!* reruns as Grampa snored in bed beside you. My brother Matt was in the shower, rap music blaring from his phone. We heard it in the main room. "She calls them butterfly shells," Dad said. "And since butterflies are fragile, she's extra careful with them." He accidentally broke off the edge of a spiraling shell he had been fiddling with, proving his point.

"But why does she like them so much?" I asked. "They're just shells."

Dad shook his head. "They're a sign of resilience," he answered. "A sign of strength in an environment where everything's trying to break it."

I never asked you what they meant to you, but as we left Miami's port that day, Mom and I sat down to talk about the beach days we'd have as well as the excursions we'd do at each island. I was determined to find you a butterfly shell at every beach we went to, so time and Mother Nature needed to be in my favor.

I didn't succeed. My mom wasn't surprised, but she told me how much she appreciated my dedication. "And she'll appreciate the effort," she said, talking about you. "You still found three. That purple one is especially gorgeous."

On our last night aboard the ship, I brought them to dinner. Pulling them from my silver clutch, I asked our head waiter to sneak them onto your dessert plate and he agreed, taking them gently from me.

Like every other night, your chocolate lava cake came out with a side of strawberry ice cream. But Ihan spun it so that the shells were right in front of you as he placed the plate down. You picked up your fork, looked down at it, and froze. The fork was slowly lowered as a small smile tipped your lips upward. Tears welled in your eyes and I felt horrible until I heard you choke out. "I've got this," you said just before you picked up the trio of shells and laid them on top of your black wallet. You went back to your lava cake, and we both spent the rest of the evening smiling to ourselves.

You passed seven months later. I tucked a butterfly shell into your casket, one I had found while touring colleges in Florida. Mom and I spent an afternoon after a tour scouring St. Pete Beach for butterfly shells. I found eight, and six survived the flight. Of the five that made it to the wake, one got lost between the funeral home and the church, and one got tossed when I emptied the tissues out of my purse. One broke in the small purse I had, but the two that endured made it to you. A white and brown one rests in the silk-lined casket with your body, while a pinkish one sits in a nook on your headstone.

Going to college in a beach town gives me ample opportunity to collect shells. It's become a ritual when I'm stressed, bored, or feeling disconnected. A ten-minute drive gets me to Pass-A-Grille, a twenty-minute drive to Upham beach with its garden in the sand. Both of these have become the spots I gather your butterfly shells, where I gather my own resilience. A small mason jar on the desk in my apartment is slowly being filled with each shell butterfly, slid in gently one by one and secured with cotton balls whenever it risks being jostled.

You may watch down from Heaven time to time, or you may have better things to do. But if little shells like these can keep it together with such a thin bond, so can I.

"Here's to the next butterfly shell," I say as I place a few more on your headstone whenever I visit.

# Benedictus

I am the woman in the green gauze gown.
My toes are webbed, my hair tangled and white.

I walk between the darkness and the light
when beach is blank and the waters ebb,

when turtles racing to the sea perish
in the moonlight as do flattened starfish

stranded by the tide. I bring blessings
from the past, from Picts and Celts, caress

the creatures with my gaze, bless the dying, free
the living, touch the wounded and weep, weep

for air no longer clear and waters red
with death, for silvery vibrance swollen on

littered shores. I walk and weep, these
beings mine to bless, no longer mine to heal.

Kaitlin Murphy-Knudsen

# Discernment

*Here a star, and there a star,*
  *Some lose their way.*

After I was wrong,
I could not order a sandwich for two years.

Under sudden waterfalls of vile words, I had prayed veils into existence.
I left, but discernment smarted too, and split.

  Volumes of affection morph into opposites
  like the manic slate of thunderclouds
  when they move across the sun—which, if you stop to look, is violent too.

  Bigger choices than sandwiches loomed.

I hunted it for years, found it waiting in a corner booth I had not seen before.
She was a sure, straight-backed woman.

What took you so long? she asked.
I sat down, and we were old friends.
*Here a mist, and there a mist,*
  *Afterwards—day!*★

Italicized portions are from Emily Dickinson's *Collected Poems* (Barnes and
Noble Books, New York, New York, 1993).

15

# Exact Change

The autumn sun in Miami Beach was just as brutal as in the summer and the thick humid air kept the streets smelling like empty beer bottles. Last night's graveyard shift at the gas station was longer than my hours of sleep but the neon green bench on Harding and Seventy-Seventh looked more worn out than me. I stood anyway, because sitting meant my clothes would get stained and I'd smell homeless. Today, I got the call I'd been waiting for.

A few months ago, my girl told me she missed her period and had taken a test; it proved positive. The next day, I'd gone to the computer lab at the North Shore Library and requested information from the U.S. Army's website about enlisting and hadn't heard back until today.

Last week we had watched as terrorists crashed planes into the Twin Towers and the Pentagon, and I guessed that had got the Army's ass in gear. The recruiter called and talked about all the advantages of signing up. After having heard half his sales pitch, I asked him for a meeting. The sergeant said to be at the recruiter's office in downtown Miami today, three o'clock sharp.

I had walked a little over half a mile to get to the K stop, which ran every hour. I wore the cleanest pair of pants I had and a collared shirt. Sweat already showed through my clothes and my thighs were chafed. After I flagged it down, a bus slowed and stopped.

The fare cost one-twenty-five. All I had was a five from selling beer after legal hours. The limp bill was crumpled in my hand. "Anyone got change?"

The driver was an old man in a dirty uniform. He wore beads with Haitian colors on his wrist. There were eight other passengers who sat far apart from one another. Most of the women wore work clothes and stared out the windows. All the men stared at the floor. The air conditioner smelled like it needed a filter change.

Not one passenger looked at me. I tried again in Spanish, but everyone pretended I didn't exist. My teeth hurt, and I thought my clenched jaw would break them.

The driver spoke up with a thick Creole accent. "Only exact change."

# ODET

There wasn't enough time to catch another K bus, and my unborn child depended on me making this appointment. I didn't want any trouble and couldn't afford it anyway. My shoulders felt like they couldn't carry even the little bit of my dignity.

I straightened the bill on the edge of the fare machine and closed my eyes. Even though I had no fare now to get back, I fed the machine my money. Staring at the LED display I said, "The next three ride free."

The driver said nothing, closed the door, and the bus rumbled forward. I sat on the empty bench with the least amount of grease spots. Decrepit apartments and motels passed me by. The gas station I worked at came into view and my girl stood behind the cash register. We'd been together since high school, but I didn't know if I could call it love. I asked my boss, an old *Marielito* Cuban, what I should do and on the down low he gave me an advance to pay for an ultrasound; he then said for us to do the right thing. We went to the clinic, and the tech had told us it was a girl.

My girl said if I couldn't support them, she'd have an abortion. Poverty terrified her, and she didn't want motherhood to be like it was for her mom in El Salvador. It was acceptable to her if it meant avoiding hunger, shame, and despair for her child. I'm not religious, but I thought it was wrong and I wanted my baby girl in this world.

There was going to be a war now. I'd seen documentaries about people enlisting to fight and the Army would take anyone who was willing and able. In exchange, they could provide a stable source of money, a job skill, and give my unborn a chance at life. Maybe I'd go to college afterward with the GI Bill. My girl had said the government took advantage of the poor, sent them to fight wars. I believed that was true, but there was no other way for us and so no reason to complain.

The bus traveled on the bridge; Miami Beach was behind, and Downtown Miami lay ahead. Traffic on the MacArthur Causeway was heavy, and I kept picking lint off my pants. Even though my stomach was empty, I felt no hunger. Doubts kept coming at me and I wondered if the traffic was a sign that this wasn't the right thing to do. Boats cruised over the water with happy people drinking and laughing. I watched the waves and passed the time daydreaming. My daughter would probably look like her mom. Her name was going to be Maria, and I'd buy a van to take her to Disney World. We'd drive home to a house in a safe neighborhood.

A few blocks from the recruiter's office, the bus stopped at a metro-rail station. Graffiti marked territories and stickers advertised nightclubs. The

Omni Mall across the street went out of business and had become a place cops wouldn't go. There was no ocean breeze here and the air stank of public transportation and unwashed bodies. I made no eye contact with the homeless while making my way. Head down, eyes up, like I'd been taught.

The early rush hour traffic on Biscayne Boulevard kept trouble off the sidewalk, but at night these corners belonged to hookers. Empty shop windows reflected the cars, and all that was left were US military recruiting stations; Uncle Sam never skipped paying the rent.

The Army office had posters of helicopters and tanks covering the storefront. The door was locked and the lights were off. According to my watch I was two minutes early. I thought back to the phone call: the recruiters had forgotten about me, there was no other explanation. My shirt stuck to my chest as I banged on the door.

At every pound of my fist the door reverberated, dangerously close to shattering the glass. From far away, I heard the desperate cry that comes from the fathers of children struck by stray bullets; I realized it was coming from me. No one was going to answer this door. My reflection in the glass fogged up and all thoughts of meeting my unborn daughter evaporated.

"Hey, knock it off."

A man in uniform had come out of the office next door. He was shorter than me and he had the wiry muscles of a street fighter. His blue pants had a red stripe along the seams. Under a colorful collection of ribbons on his tan short-sleeve shirt, a black name tag spelled Gonzalez. The rank on his sleeves were strange, like the Army's but with crossed rifles in the middle.

I stuttered, "I had a meeting and they aren't there."

He said nothing and went back inside. The door had an eagle, globe, and anchor, with the words United States Marine Corps above. I stood up as straight as I could and followed him.

The streets were behind me and a wave of cold air conditioning covered my sweat-slick skin. There were three other Marines, each one on the phone. They all wore the same uniform as the other man, but with different ranks and ribbons.

When the door closed, the man I had seen outside waited with his arms crossed and said, "Can I help you?"

"My name is Juan Carlos. I was looking for the Army guys." My hand hung in the air for a heartbeat.

His calloused grip nearly crushed my hand, and he smiled after he caught me wincing. "I'm Gunny Gonzalez. We don't know where they are, and we don't care."

"Oh." I didn't understand his disrespect toward the Army recruiters, but I shared it.

Gunny asked, "Are you looking to join?"

I nodded and put my hands in empty pockets.

"That's good." He took a step toward me and I stood firm. "Have you considered other branches?"

I lied, "Yes."

The Marine gestured behind him. "Oh really, have you considered the Marines?"

My tongue felt too big for my mouth. "I . . . well . . ."

He sized me up from my worn-out Chuck Taylors. "Oh, it's too tough for you, Juan Carlos?"

My girl wasn't going to wait much longer. After I'd figured out how to swallow again, I said, "Alright, show me what the Marines are about, sir."

He clapped my shoulder. "Outstanding. Call me Gunny, not sir."

Gunny crooked a finger toward a stocky recruiter with biceps as wide as my thighs. He hung up the phone and moved as fast as a linebacker chasing down a quarterback. Gunny told him, "Sergeant Travino, this is Juan Carlos, and he wants to see what we got."

After I exchanged handshakes with the sergeant, Gunny went into an office with a doorframe but no door. Travino led me to a small room with a couch opposite a TV/VCR on a rolling cart. Posters with grim looking men in combat fatigues decorated almost every bit of white space. Bumper stickers with phrases like *Pain is Weakness Leaving the Body*, and *The Few, the Proud, the Marines*, were on almost every piece of furniture. He rewound a VHS tape and pushed play. He said, "When this is finished, come to my desk."

A marching drumbeat opened the video. I sat back, thankful to be out of the humid air, and listened to the deep baritone voice on the screen. The words he spoke were of honor, courage, commitment, and being the best. Clips showed young men and women running out of swimming tanks, rappelling from hovering helicopters, and firing guns like I'd seen in *Rambo* and *Apocalypse Now*. There was a litany of historical battles recited with reverence, a scene of a Marine pulling up to a barracks in a Mustang, then a family living in a house on base next to a playground. The video concluded with crossed American and Marine Corps flags.

I hardly blinked the entire time. They offered what I needed but wanted me to be willing to do things like on the tape. By the time all my sweat had dried, my mind was made up. Making sure no one saw me, I made the sign of the cross before leaving the TV behind.

Travino was at his desk. There were two empty chairs across and I sat in the one directly in front of him. He was on the phone speaking in Spanish and held up a finger when he looked up at me from his paperwork. After placing the receiver on the hook, he said, "The problem with Miami is no one here can pass the ASVAB composition portion. You speak good English?"

"Yes."

He penciled notes on an index card and placed it on a pile. "What'd you think of the video?"

"I'm in. I'll sign up."

"Just like that, huh? Well not so fast. Let's do a pre-ASVAB, see where you are," From his desk, he grabbed a stapled packet of papers and slammed the drawer shut, and a Marine made me flinch for the second time. Sergeant Travino stood and motioned with his head to follow.

There was a small desk at the back of the office. It had the same look as the cheap ones in school, fake wood with a veneer of quality. I sat and faced a poster that had three men coming up from a jungle river holding rifles. He handed me a pencil and the test.

With a few beeps, Travino set his digital timer and set it down. "You have an hour. Do your best to answer all the questions. You don't lose points for guessing."

He walked away, probably to make more calls. The test looked like it was a copy of a copy, worn out and slightly off kilter. There were multiple choices and it covered math, reading comprehension, grammar, and mechanics. My high school GPA was a solid two-point-two, and I'd never been good with machines either, didn't even own a car, so I Christmas tree'd my way through. After the timer went off, I circled the last answer, got up, and stood in front of his desk while he finished on the phone.

He hung up like he was dropping a loaded barbell. "Fuck, that's it for today." The rest of the office was empty, except for Gunny's.

I placed the test and the pencil on his desk, next to a dog-eared packet that was the answer key. "Finished."

He grabbed the papers and said, "You sure?"

He didn't wait for a response and graded me. I did not expect him to smile, but that is what happened. In a practiced light tone, he said, "Have a seat, Juan Carlos."

My voice wavered. "How did I do?"

He tossed the test my way. There were about as many check marks as x's, "You scored well enough. This is not an official score, but usually we want potential recruits to study . . ."

I interrupted, "When can I take the real thing?"

He raised his palm like he was stopping traffic. "What's the rush?"

My truth was too small and worthless to him. I told him a grand lie that he'd value. "I don't want to miss out on the war."

Travino nodded as if we shared an understanding. "Why do you want to join?"

The words from the video tape came to mind and I said what he wanted to hear, "To serve my country."

After leaning back, he placed a green notebook on his desk and said, "I have a couple of others I'm taking tomorrow morning to Miami MEPS for the ASVAB. I can pick you up."

I laughed like I'd just won a scratch-off lotto ticket. "Thank you."

"Don't thank me yet. Let's fill out some paperwork first. After the real test, we can talk ship dates and jobs." He drew out papers with official government letterheads and began writing in the designated boxes. Maria was going to be born.

"One question."

Travino stopped filling out the form and met my eyes. "Shoot."

"Can I bum bus fare from you guys?"

*The Traveler*, Arthur Doweyko

*Almost Home*, Arthur Doweyko

# Dark and Empty

I saw her on the news last night
The mother of that dead girl
She looked so calm and peaceful
And spoke without a tremble

The mother of that dead girl
The picture of composure
Spoke without a tremble
Of her lovely daughter's life

A picture of composure
She smiled into the camera
Her lovely daughter's life
Still as real to her as ever

She smiled into the camera
But her eyes were dark and empty
Still as real to her as ever
She felt her daughter's presence

Though her eyes were dark and empty
She looked so calm and peaceful
She still felt her daughter's presence
When I saw her on the news

*Written the day after the mass shooting at Marjory Stoneman High School in Parkland, Florida*

# The Lost Saint

"When you're young," Bud once told me, "you visit your family doctor as a friend. He takes your blood pressure and asks you what's going on in your life. Then he tells you about his new dog or his fishing trip. On the other side of sixty, around the time you sign up for Medicare, every time you go for a check-up, he finds things wrong with you."

Our neighbor's doctor stopped being a friend when he told Bud that his hoarseness and annoying cough were symptoms of lung cancer. He hadn't smoked for five years—not since his brother died of a heart attack, but the damage had been done.

"Maybe I'll take up the habit again," he said. "What can it hurt?" Of course we discouraged that train of thought and knew he was just pushing our buttons.

Bud was a churchgoer but not a Bible banger, and I always enjoyed his folksy wisdom as we talked over the split-rail fence that divided our properties. He chatted about God as though the Creator was just another neighbor. "The cypress head was calling for rain, and I guess the Good Lord heard," he'd say, as we eyed the gathering clouds. If he didn't have a new story to tell each time he saw me, he'd make one up.

He wasn't exactly a dog-whisperer, but it was obvious that he had a way with animals and a need to nurture them. Horses, cats, dogs—even a feral hog—found homes on his plot of rural Florida. He loved them almost as much as he loved his grandchildren.

When we first moved next to his twelve acres, his family's pet-of-the-year was an old Saint Bernard named Heidi, who rarely left Bud's side. While Bud carried on a conversation or was simply lost in thought, he'd give no special attention to the dog beyond burying his hand in her thick coat. Heidi would stare at Bud with dark, trusting eyes. Over several years, we watched her coat grow thin, her gait grow slow. Although she wasn't replaced when she died, Bud sent regular donations to a Saint Bernard rescue foundation. I always thought it odd that the breed honored for rescuing people in the snowy Alps sometimes needed to be rescued themselves.

Meanwhile, on Bud's farm, a menagerie of other dogs collected, as people, with no qualms at all, abandoned unwanted canines on his property.

25

Mixed-breed terriers and dachshunds followed closely at Bud's heels as he fed steers, repaired fencing, or picked oranges. As his cancer progressed and his footsteps faltered, they threatened to trip him, but he seemed to rally in their company. The dogs were Bud's pals.

Over the space of a few months, we couldn't help but notice that Bud was getting smaller. I was patient when conversations over the fence were interrupted by fits of crusty coughing. Pain and exhaustion wrinkled his face, and eventually the disease took such complete hold of him that he no longer left the house. Whenever I visited, the lethargic dog-pack lay by the back door, waiting for Bud to come outside.

My neighbor's life ended suddenly, on a rainy evening in June when his wife was at their married daughter's house, shucking corn for the freezer.

When sheriff's cruisers arrived and parked in the grass along their driveway, we learned that Bud had put the barrel of a revolver into his mouth and taken his life. Bud's four grown children and their families quickly gathered at his house. We kept our distance, respecting their privacy.

The next morning, I went over there, toting a baked ham and wondering what I would say. Yellow crime scene ribbons surrounded the house. I entered the kitchen where Bud's wife sat at the table he'd built. I could see she was trying to make sense of it.

"I couldn't do anything for him." Lottie sighed. Her eyes swung side-to-side, as though they were seeing, once more, all the events leading up to the grisly scene that had met her when she came home. "He'd always panic when he couldn't breathe. He'd wave me away, so I wouldn't see him gasping. He told me he'd be okay when Beth asked me to come and help her with the corn."

While she had been pouring corn kernels into freezer-bags, Bud was at home, spreading a plastic shower curtain across the bed they had shared for over forty years. He had settled himself onto the curtain, attempting to create an impossibly peaceful scene, with no mess for her to clean. He had underestimated the gory sight she encountered.

Now Lottie was telling the story over and over, adding new details as they came to mind, hoping to explain why Bud had made that final decision.

Others in Lottie's kitchen continued to listen to her grim recitings, but I walked out the back door, afraid that I, meaning to console her, might awkwardly say the wrong thing. Bud had placed all of us smack in the middle of a tragedy. The thought of his desperation sickened me. Would I have stopped him, had I known, expecting him to endure unknown days of torment while his family watched? He knew the inevitable was near. Suicide burdens friends and family with guilt, but what could any of us have said or done for him? I figured that his life—and his death—meant a lot more to him than they did to me. He'd made his choice.

As I left the house and entered the yard, Bud's mutts were yapping, roused from their nap in the tall, summertime grass. The pack began running down the dirt drive, toward a large, shaggy shape that was lumbering toward us.

The Saint Bernard was matted and filthy—a dog quite different from the yappy little beasts that were dropped out of cars by thoughtless owners. He approached the welcoming committee, and they, in return, nosed his behind for proper identification. Satisfied that he was a male, but not aggressive, they set their tails to wagging mode and trotted beside him, up the drive to a picnic table under the oaks, where Bud's five grandchildren were sitting, uncommonly quiet and missing their granddad. The Saint Bernard hunkered down beside them in the shade. His dry tongue hung from his mouth, and he was panting as though he had traveled far to reach this destination.

One of the children brought a pan of water, and while the dog drank, the others began to remove sticks and leaves from his tangled hair. In our country neighborhood, we know all the resident animals. This one was a homeless stranger. While he might have headed up any dirt drive to any house, including ours, he had passed them by and picked this one.

Bud's eldest son Cory emerged from the house, and the children dragged him to the dog.

"This guy's come a long way," Cory said, inspecting him. "His foot pads are torn up. And whoever owned him didn't treat him too good. He's got no tag, and he's scarred from old wounds. He's got some new sores, too."

I found some Purina chow in the shed, and we watched as the lost Saint hungrily devoured a bowlful.

Someone suggested a bath, and the youngest cousins, looking for an escape from the sorrow that weighed so heavily on them, pulled out a garden hose. Gently, they washed the dog's wounds, sudsing away dried blood and dirt. The lost Saint stood quietly while the children, with surprising cooperation and refreshing laughter, rinsed and rinsed, then dried him with old beach towels.

Over the next couple days they lavished love on the dog they began to call *Buddy-Boy*. They applied ointment to his wounded feet and brushed his coat. He licked them gratefully.

The dog hung around and eventually moved into the house with Lottie. After Bud's funeral, the family searched Facebook pages and classified ads of the newspaper for "lost dog" appeals without success. They tacked signs to poles, but no owner claimed him. Of course, we all recalled Bud's fondness for Saint Bernards, and because we needed reassurance that Bud had attained the peace he sought and the freedom from pain he deserved, we were ready to believe any sign that spoke to us. The dog's presence rescued us from our grief. Bud was okay. He had to be okay.

# 'Fraidy Hole

1975,
we lied
to the born-again

neighbor's boy
that a kid died there.

He wanted to see.
We threatened him

not to bring his sister.
It was out of bounds,

farther than when streetlights
went off, an earthen hole

in a construction site
eaten out by a John Deere

whose keys were stolen by bullies
we knew to be wary of.

Sean Casey boasted it was deeper
than the deep-end in the adults' pool.

I caught its bottom smell:
soaked cardboard and rugs.

Then lordy-boy lied—
heard his mother calling.

Jeff cursed him 'fraidy cat.
I needed someone to go down.

Adolescence is a spurring pandemic.
Go down, or we'd push you down.

Spur me to collect the black necklace of pollywog
that rims the pond;

spurred on by roadkill guts;
the barefoot kid I spurred on past
the broken glass in a tunnel on the creek—

spurred by the chest of the girl whose shirt I pulled up;
the scab on the weird boy's arm

that he ate on a dare;
go down or we'd push you down.

Tolstoy wrote that all the land
any person really needs is a hole 6x6.

# California or Burst

When I was fourteen I hitchhiked from Columbus to Portland. Alone. The year was 1949 and though things were different then, I still wonder how my parents allowed me to go. My father dropped me off at the corner of Broad and High Streets. I had a small cardboard suitcase and $35. I went for two reasons—I wanted to see mountains and I wanted to visit several relatives I had never seen.

By luck the first person who picked me up was going all the way to Yellowstone. His job was to open the service station at the northwestern entrance to the park. I mostly slept through Kansas, but was wide awake in Colorado when I saw the faint outlines of the Rockies. I marveled at Cheyenne. I expected a city, but the main street could not have been more than a mile long with perhaps a dozen side streets. I'd estimate the population at five thousand. Today's tourist town of Jackson Hole was then a cowboy town. The streets were dirt, the sidewalks wooden, and the parking spots were for horses.

Yellowstone opened the first of June and the man, Bill, was to be there by the second. We arrived on time, in the late afternoon. Most of the roads had been plowed, but there was deep snow everywhere. After getting the place ready to open the next day, we drove just over the line to Gardiner, Montana, a town of perhaps five hundred with several restaurants and bars. We chose one and ordered supper. It was there I saw my first slot machine. It took only silver dollars and I had none and no money to spare, but Bill dropped ten dollars.

I slept in the barracks that night. The next morning there was no breakfast and it was snowing.

Most of my clothing was warm-weather type but I was wearing work shoes, a light jacket, and a ball cap. Bill had a ranger drop me off at a junction where Route 30 led out of the park over to West Yellowstone.

It was snowing and I was shivering. Although the park had just officially opened, no cars were on the roads. I had been there an hour when I heard rustling in the brush about a hundred yards down the road. Within a few seconds a black bear and two cubs broke through the underbrush moving at a good clip. Well, I didn't know a black bear from a green one. All I knew was BEAR heading toward me.

At that precise moment, a 1947 blue Chrysler sedan rounded the curve. I assume the driver saw me and the bears and stopped. The bears were gaining. There were two old people in the front, two in the back. I crammed my suitcase between the two old people in the rear, climbed in, and sat atop it. No ride has ever been more appreciated.

They dropped me off in West Yellowstone. It had stopped snowing, the sun came out, and the ice on the roads began to melt. I found a restaurant, had breakfast, and hit the road.

A salesman from Los Angeles in a Ford coupe picked me up. He was headed home, in a hurry. Winter was grudgingly giving way to spring, but the roads had not been fixed and the potholes were frequent and deep. Didn't stop the salesman—must have been after his wife or girlfriend. He flew and never dodged a pothole. When we got to Pocatello, he had to get four tires and two rims. While we were waiting on the car to be fixed, we found a diner. He ordered a steak with the fixings. I ordered a hamburger and a glass of milk.

"Aren't you hungry?" he asked.

"I'm watching my money," I replied.

"Here," he said, "give the kid the same thing I'm having."

"How do you want your steak?" asked the cook.

Well, I had never eaten a steak that my mother hadn't prepared. "Done," I declared.

After supper we got the car and filled the gas tank. "Can you drive?" the salesman asked.

"Sure," I replied.

"Do you have a license?"

"Sure," I replied.

I wasn't lying. I did have a license but it was no good in Idaho. Back then in Ohio, one could get a restricted license at age 14, and I had one. Thing is, it was restricted to Ohio. But do you think I was going to give up a chance to drive through the Rocky Mountains at night? Not on your life.

Things went well. I stopped to get gas once. The salesman paid the bill and slept on.

Morning began to break; I was really sleepy. We were out of the twists and turns but still at a high altitude. The road was fairly straight with deep ditches on each side, the terrain mostly level.

I did not want to give up the wheel, but I couldn't keep my eyes open.

I closed them and went to sleep. I suppose the sounds associated with driving in the ditch woke me up. I whipped the wheel to the left and came zooming out of the ditch.

The salesman flew from the back and landed someplace between the front seat and the dashboard. "Are you sleepy?"

"Yeah," I said.

"Maybe I'd better drive!"

"Yeah."

We stopped for breakfast and when we got back inside the car, I was out in a New York second and did not awaken until we came to a junction—a junction where he was going one way and I, another.

It didn't take long to get a ride, but it was only for a couple of miles. Then a man in a jeep picked me up and went about a half mile, where he took a side road. I was in the middle of nowhere, with fir trees all about and a saw mill a few hundred feet behind me, doing business. I was there the rest of the day, which seemed liked ten hours and probably was. A fellow stopped and said he was going to Carson City. I didn't care if he was going to France—I got in.

It was near dusk when we stopped at a small wooden hotel. I got a room on the second floor for three bucks. This was the only time I was homesick. I didn't have a road map, as such. What I had was a large map of the United States. I unfolded it and it covered most of the bed. I found Carson City and then Columbus and thought they were mighty far apart. I was at the south end of town and after supper I walked to the other end and back. It didn't take long; it was a small town.

Next day, my first ride took me south of Lake Tahoe and then southwest into California. My second and last ride of the day came from an Idaho State student. He was done for the year and heading home to Modesto. My suitcase had the words "Miami U" on the side. My older brother, Kacy, had taped them on when he was a student at Miami of Ohio and hitchhiked back and forth. So, I decided to pass myself off as a college student. Even at five-ten and a hundred and sixty-five I'm certain he saw through me. When he asked what I was studying, I answered "Business administration," as I knew that was what Kacy was taking.

He was by far the nicest person who picked me up. We had a great afternoon of conversation. He was in the college of forestry and his father had recently passed away. When we arrived in Modesto it was late afternoon and he asked me if I wanted to stay the night. Of course I accepted. I met his mother, had a great supper and a good night's rest.

Next morning after breakfast, he took me to the edge of town headed toward San Francisco, wished me good luck, and left me off. There was a huge sign over the road that read, "Welcome to Modesto. Home of Health, Wealth and Water." I don't know about the health and the wealth, but there was not a body of water within a hundred miles of that place.

I spent several hours before that sign. It must have been a hundred degrees and I was dying of thirst—give me some of that water! Late in the afternoon, an old man in an old car picked me up. He was going to Oakland. He'd driven out to do some fishing and was headed home. It was a two-lane road and he drove about thirty—sometimes it was more like twenty-five. Every hour or so he'd pull onto the berm, take a leak, and sit on the running board and drink a beer. After each beer he would drive a little slower. It was very hot and he'd get to sweating. He'd pull out a faded red bandana and wipe his brow. This went on all the way to Oakland and I can honestly say he was never drunk. And I can honestly say it was pitch dark when we arrived. I think he realized I would never be able to get a ride at that time of night so he drove me to the bus station in San Francisco and let me off.

I caught the bus to my destination which was Santa Rosa, fifty miles north, then a town of about ten thousand. It was two or so in the morning when I arrived. My aunts, uncles, and cousins didn't know I was coming, so I waited until morning to call my Aunt Edith. To say the least, she was surprised.

My Santa Rosa family was from my mother's side, most of whom I had never seen. Her brother, Fred, his wife Grace, their children Chandler (Buzzy) and Laurel. Grace was America's best cook. Fred, mid-forties, was a chauffer and gardener for Joe Grace, owner of Grace Brother's Beer. Laurel was fifteen and Buzzy, seventeen, had a driver's license. They were still in school so I rode around town on Buzzy's Cushman motor scooter. My favorite destination was an ice cream parlor that featured Green River milkshakes. I don't know what they consisted of but they were the world's best.

Joe Grace's wife was in the hospital in Sacramento. Uncle Fred would drive him down where he would stay in a hotel a few days to visit his wife. His estate took up a whole city block, that is to say, there was a street on all four sides. His was the first place I had ever seen that had wall-to-wall carpeting.

Mom's sister, Edith, also lived in Santa Rosa along with her husband Joe. Their daughter, Bonnie, was five. Edith was my favorite aunt and Joe my favorite uncle. Joe was wounded in WWII and sent to our house in Sunbury, Ohio to recuperate. Edith came by train to be with Joe.

They stayed with us until Joe had to return to war. Aunt Edith stayed in Sunbury until the war ended; therefore, I got to know her well and loved her dearly.

I also had family in Oregon. Mom's sister, Aunt Lillian Kendig, her husband, Fritz, and cousins Max, Don and Jim.

It was decided that Buzzy would accompany me to Portland (actually Oregon City) to watch over me. Really, I took care of him. We rode several hundred miles with a trucker to Eureka. He was pulling a flat-bed on which we sat, dangling our legs over the back at 60 m.p.h. We had Uncle Joe's WWII down-feather sleeping bag back there. After we stopped to eat, we found it gone. Either it had fallen off or someone swiped it, so we were down to my bed roll which proved sufficient.

Our visit with the Kendigs was wonderful—cool crisp weather and places to see. Max was special; as a junior he was the state heavyweight wrestling champion. As a senior he would become an all-state football player and heavyweight champion again in wrestling. He and I got along great. He was my favorite cousin and still is, even though he's been dead ten years.

Eventually, it became time to go back to Santa Rosa. We decided to go through eastern Oregon which is desert-like—hot, dry, and crummy. We'd been hitchhiking for hours beside a dusty road when a man in a coupe picked us up. We put our stuff in the back and the three of us rode in front.

After a long drive, the driver spotted a car at a restaurant. "That's a friend of mine," he said. "We'll stop there and eat."

Sure enough he knew the guy and they were headed for the same place, so after lunch the driver of our car said, "It's crowded in my car with the three of us. Why don't one of you ride with me and the other go with so and so?"

I didn't want to separate but eventually we did.

Within a few minutes, the other car was out of sight and I had a bad feeling in my stomach. It grew a lot worse when my driver reached under his seat, pulled out a handgun, and laid it by his side.

*Oh, shit!* I said to myself. *He's going to kill me, the other guy is going to kill Buzzy and bury both of us in the desert.*

What he didn't know was that I had a four- or five-inch hunting knife attached to my belt, hidden inside my shorts with a T-shirt covering it. I aimed to go down fighting. I unsnapped the leather catch and put my hand on the hilt. We drove for miles, neither talking.

Then without looking he reached slowly for the gun and wrapped his hand around the butt. For several minutes his hand lay there. I watched his hand out of the corner of my eye. The muscles in his hand contracted. At the same time my hand did too. He started to lift the gun. I started to pull the knife. He lifted the gun. I lifted the knife.

Just when I thought he was going to shoot me, he pointed the gun out the window and blasted away at a road sign. I let out a sigh of relief that could be heard in Columbus.

Late that afternoon, we arrived at a junction where we were going one way, they another. Once we were alone, I related my story to Buzzy and we decided never to split again.

The next day, we arrived back in Santa Rosa with the safety and comfort of home.

Did I learn anything? You bet your sweet bippy.

I took the Greyhound home.

Left to right: Max Kendig, 16, Author Roy Ault, 14, Chandler (Buzzy) Goodrich, 17.

*Picture taken at the Kendig home, Gladstone, OR, 1948.*

# Home

Coming home, when the water line ebbs
and tropical depressions weigh down air,
sponges of New Orleans humidity
and swamp-wrung skin;
even after the tornado ripped the roof
off your house,
      and you,
stooped on hands and knees to scrub your dresser,
wheezing against dust into the crook of your arm,
hold your breath to scrub your moldy bed before
ripping out dry wall, scraping blood and dirt
from tattered fingernails
with stacks of childhood photos
      rotting.
Friends ask,
Why bother to return?
But you gaze in home's gray pothole eyes
leaking into streets, shallow Lake Pontchartrain
cheekbones and flat face a crumbled levee,
vowing
      you will always go back for her.

# Pride (Noun)

I attend my first real Pride event in St. Petersburg, Florida. It's so hot out, my glasses fog up as I exit my studio and start the five-block walk to my best friend's house. I'm sweating by the time I get there. It stays with me even as I sit in her kitchen, the air conditioning drying me into a plaster.

I sip a glass of tequila on ice, fanning myself. Tonight starts a weekend of events, some of which will have thousands of people in attendance. This is new for me. I haven't participated in anything like it since coming out at twenty-five.

The event tonight is a fashion show, so I wear a skin tight white jumpsuit that slits open to the bottom of my breastbone. It's unlike me—I'm usually prudish. While I'll wear crop tops, I never wear anything low cut. I'm hesitant to wear anything that might bring me attention; it overwhelmingly comes from straight men.

After feeding the dogs, my friends and I take a Lyft to the show, only a few blocks away in downtown St. Pete. It's inside the fine arts museum and when we arrive, the smell of food hangs in the air. The museum looks so different. Banners and silver decorations flutter, suspended from the ceiling. The lights flicker, dim, and two bars line the sides of the room. A runway rests where the café usually sits. People stand crammed together in line, gesturing, mouths opening and closing.

I don't do well with crowds. After meeting up with some other friends, I immediately go to the bar for a drink. There's so much going on, it's hard for me to focus. Voices rise and fall in the room. My neck is tight. Finally, the bartender hands me a ginger and whiskey. I've just taken my first sip when a man in a sharp, gray suit leans in and says, "My God, honey. You are the hottest person here."

Warmth flushes my chest. "Shut up," I say. Then quieter, "Thank you."

Throughout the show, several other attendees comment on how good my outfit looks. I'm shocked and pleased. I'm not used to compliments, at least, none like this. Not the kind that come from a peer, someone who recognizes me as a woman, not as an object, but as a person in power of her sexuality.

Most of my time is spent in straight spaces. At work, I'm surrounded by straight women. I spend eight hours a day with them but none of them ever really see me. I'm cute to them. Adorable, even. They coddle me like they would a child.

Intermittently throughout the show I text Emma, a girl I've liked for several months now. I report on the mutual acquaintances we have here and tell her about the decorations and outfits the models are wearing. She says she wishes she could be there. Her texts make her sound excited but tired, different from how she was when we first started talking and she used to text me in big, long paragraphs, telling me how much she liked me, how excited she was to see me. *I missed you today,* she'd say. *I like getting to see you after work even if it's only for a little bit.*

The fashion show picks up. The outfits get more and more revealing and my friends and I clap louder and louder as the sun starts to set outside. I spend the rest of the night willing myself not to text Emma and enjoying the compliments I get from other attendees. When the show is finally over, I surprise myself by not wanting to leave.

★ ★ ★

At work the next day, I speed through grant applications, reviewing budgets and sitting in the sunshine that pours in through the window next to my desk. I ride the high from the fashion show until I get home and receive a text from a woman who is also close with Emma. The air conditioner hisses in the background. My stomach grows tight as I sit down and open the text.

*Emma's back with Charlie!*

My brain catches fire. Charlie? The guy who threw a pizza on her floor once while having a tantrum? Tension sweeps my body. I put the phone down, but I'm not really that shocked. Looking back, I could see the signs. I just got excited, and didn't want to acknowledge them. *Wow,* I type back. *That's going to be interesting.*

*So interesting,* she says.

I put my phone down. I'm attending a trans pride night later and from the tightness in my chest and neck, I already know it's going to be a struggle. My whole body is buzzing. I go to the refrigerator, immediately take out a can of beer and suck it back. It goes straight to my head and neck but does little to ease the pain.

Sitting in front of my laptop, staring at an empty screen, I tell myself I'm not going to get upset. Emma was never my girlfriend. We've only been talking for a few months. What did I expect?

After drinking two more beers, I leave the house and spend the evening with friends sipping IPAs in the warehouse of a local brewery. It's warm inside and the sounds of our voices echo up to the ceiling, dozens of feet high. The beers are sharp and cold. I meet a bunch of new people, chatting about advocacy and some new educational programs I want to spearhead, but as the night wears on, my energy wanes.

My friends want to leave, so we all pile in the car and head downtown. We've got the windows down and the music turned up when all of a sudden, I'm exhausted. I'm done celebrating Pride. I'm done pretending to be happy. While coming out has saved my life in many ways, it's also felt like a curse. My straight friends are all married and happy; I'm still searching. Since coming out, I've tried hard to open myself up for love, even though my pool is incredibly small now. That possibility has opened the door to rejection and that rejection means having to say goodbye to women I've come to truly care about, over and over again.

We arrive in the park and I let everyone know I'm going for food, then start walking downtown. I slip my earbuds in and make my way to a 24-hour diner just a few blocks away. There's no one inside, but the lights are on high and the smell of cooking grease wafts through the space. I take a seat at one of the booths and look through the menu.

When the waiter approaches, I order avocado with fried egg and a side of home fries, then eat quickly. I read through a friend's story on my phone, then pause to look out the wall-length window next to the booth. Outside, a woman sits with her daughter at a metal table and chairs. The mother has frizzy, spiral hair, and her daughter's is exactly the same. They share a sandwich, picking at a plate of sweet potato fries between them. The girl laughs, and I'm struck by a loneliness that's so familiar, I barely notice as it overtakes me.

I finish eating quickly and pay my tab. Outside, the night sky is filled with ambient light from the city, too light to see the stars. I walk the mile home with my hands in my pockets, music loud in my ears, and when I get home, I curl up in my bed and cry until I fall asleep.

★ ★ ★

When I graduated from middle school, I cried for days. I didn't want to go to high school. It was four miles further from my house and I'd have all new teachers. My entire way of life was being uprooted. I cried and cried, wishing I could find a way to stay just a little bit longer.

While I blamed my anguish on losing comfort and familiarity, the heart of it was a red-haired teacher with freckles, a loud personality, and oversized glasses. She had a biting sense of humor and was short but thick with curves. I thought about her all the time. Going to her classes made life brighter.

I wrote her letters that I never sent and returned to my middle school on two different occasions, hoping to say hello but never finding her. I lost track of her about halfway through high school, when I started liking another teacher.

Then about a year and a half ago, I saw my red-haired teacher walking down the street in the state capital where I grew up. I stopped her, touching her shoulder, and it took her several seconds to recognize me. Her eyes grew big and she smiled. She was heavier than I remembered, and her face had aged in the fifteen years since we'd last seen each other. I could see her looking at mine, assessing the damage—the drinks, the issues I had with my mental health. "It's so amazing to see you," she said.

I smiled. "We should get a drink sometime."

"We should."

"You've been well?"

"I'm so good," she said.

I looked down at her and tried to summon that heartfelt emotion I'd once had for her, but it had fled, replaced by this bewildered apathy, this confusion and deep sadness over no longer being able to feel what I'd felt for her. The spark was gone. Disappeared somewhere. Now we were no one to each other.

That was the part I hated about liking people. Some would never really see you, no matter how hard you tried, and the spark would never have anywhere to go. So much hope and heart and passion, all to burn out.

For me, that was the saddest thing of all.

★ ★ ★

I make it through the Pride parade the next day without drinking too much and wake up in the morning surprisingly not hungover. The sun is shining and a coat of humidity lines the glass panels of my front door. After getting ready, I step outside. It's quarter of nine and already the heat bugs hiss. The organization I work for has rented a booth at the Pride street festival and I'm the event planner, so I'll be working it all day in the heat. Even in the first few minutes of being outside, I can feel the prickle of sweat beading along my skin—on my neck, my back. Everywhere.

By the time I get to the booth and unpack with a few of my coworkers, I'm ready for the day to be over. The sun beats down on us. I hide under trees and in the lip of shade provided by our small tent.

"Jesus fucking Christ," I say to one of my coworkers.

She wipes her face with her t-shirt. "Jesus has no place in this hell hole."

After setting up, I sit for a moment and drink some water. My body starts to cool down, while around me, the street fair picks up. I love watching everyone in their outfits. I love looking up all the different Pride flags and reading people's shirts. It's a joyful thing to see so many young people in the streets, confident and sure of themselves.

As the day wears on, a few friends visit my booth. My coworkers switch shifts. I take blue raspberry Jell-O shots with them and talk about work, but there is this thing inside of me that's blank all day, unable to muster any of the joy everyone else is experiencing.

Pride is supposed to be a celebration. But how can I celebrate something that has brought so much darkness into my life? I want to be the girl that wraps a lesbian flag around my shoulders and paints rainbows on my cheeks and shouts at the whole world exactly who I am. But how? I haven't figured out how to love this identity yet. While I love the validation and support I get from queer spaces, sometimes affirming my queerness means accepting a part of my life that has been filled with great sadness.

Finally, the vendors around us start packing up and I follow suit, taking down the tent and wrapping up our leftover swag. My skin is coated in dried sweat. I want to take a shower. I want to be somewhere quiet and dark.

One of my coworkers helps me pack all our things into a small wagon. She wears a bi flag around her shoulders like a superhero cape. The colors— pink, purple, blue—shimmer in the light. "That's pretty," I say.

She grabs the handle of our cooler. "Gotta let them know somehow."

"It's too hot for capes," I say. "Just paint the word GAY on my forehead."

She laughs, and we roll our stuff into the parking lot, hiding under the shade of the tree as our ride pulls up, spewing dust into the air. We labor, hefting boxes into the trunk before cramming into the empty seats. As we drive away, I want to tell my coworker that I envy her. I envy how excited she was to find her flag earlier and how she put it on with so much pride. How she still has it on now, even though we're beyond the crowd.

After first coming out, I had this incredible excitement over finally being able to be myself. That slowly turned to frustration as I failed and failed and failed with women, and then it turned to fear. Now, that fear is long gone. It's just this quiet surrender, this acceptance of how the cards may fall for me, how they've fallen for many who have lived before me.

"Happy Pride," the girl with the bi-flag says as we reach her car and stop to drop her off. She climbs out, then turns to us, smiling and waving.

I wave, the sunlight glinting as I force a smile back. "Happy Pride, love."

# My Teeth Were Eaten

My teeth were eaten
by your teeth;
my tongue removed
by your tongue.
You pulled off my toes
and stuck them on another me.
I was most happy
to be reassembled.
The first thing I felt
when you arrived?
My teeth hurt so bad
I wanted to bite something,
I wanted to gnaw
through the wall keeping me in.

Patricia Blauvelt

# Childhood Home

Wedged in a middle seat on a plane leaving Miami, I introduced myself to the two passengers bookending me and talked non-stop, whiplashing my head as if I was at a tennis game, all to hide my nervousness. No, I wasn't scared of flying. I was afraid of going home. The ninety-minute flight crossed the ocean to my birthplace after I left it three decades before. I wanted to step on its ground and relive the remnants of a care-free, simple and idyllic life. That house had sheltered me in its bosom at the most impressionable phase of my life.

I left Haiti in 1973 to join my parents in America in search of a better life. My physical body made the move, but my heart took a few years to follow. I set out to enrich my mind and my pockets and return home. I never wanted to be a permanent resident of the United States. Then I became an American citizen.

Before I was born, my parents built our four-room house, one room at a time in a community settled on leased land owned by a wealthy Haitian family. By the time I came along as the middle child of seven, the house was completed. Like all the others around it, it had no electricity or indoor plumbing, but it was the biggest in the neighborhood. It was my castle.

In the morning, the sun would step through the wide window of my bedroom like an invited guest, bringing in the beginning of adventure and the sounds of free-range chickens, pigs and goats. The early morning breeze caressed my face like gentle fingers, waking me up to the smell of Grandma's coffee. I licked my lips wishing I could drink the brew. I stepped over my sleeping sister in the bed and like I did every morning, I said, "Grandma, when can I have coffee?"

She smiled. "When you're old enough to vote, Child."

"But . . . no one votes here." I shook my head and squatted next to her in the small outdoor kitchen. The acrid smell of the burning charcoal tickled my throat, making me want the coffee even more. "Yesterday my friend Marie said we live in a dictatorship," I whispered.

Grandma put her cup down. Hot coffee splashed on the ground. She squeezed my hand hard and whispered back, "Don't ever say that word in this house again."

"What . . . what does it mean?"

"Nothing," she said, nudging me with her shoulder. "Go get ready for school."

In the afternoon, I roamed the neighborhood after finishing my homework, chasing my siblings, my cousins and my friends around until the songs of the night creatures carried me home exhausted but happy.

At night, the flickering flames from the kerosene lamps splashed our disjointed shadows on the cement walls. We gyrated, throwing our arms over our heads as we pretended to be puppets being pulled by strings in a joyful dance. Sitting on the floor around my grandmother for our nightly ritual of storytelling and lullaby singing, I felt the embrace of the walls like hugs.

Frequently my parents took in relatives who came from the countryside. They stayed with us for as long as they needed. That was the custom. So, the house bustled with people and activities all the time. When I complained about the lack of space, Grandma would say, "A home is elastic when it comes to family. There's always room."

I shared one of the bedrooms with my three sisters, my grandmother and any female relative visiting at the time. The bougainvillea my father planted grew on a trellis that formed a welcoming arch to our red painted front door. The sea-green exterior walls and white trims on the window frames gave the house a happy aura, just like its residents. That red door stayed open from dawn to dusk like open arms to shelter and nourish the weary traveler or burdened neighbor.

Then in 1970 my parents emigrated to America. I mourned the void left by their departure and the inevitable change that would occur in my life, when I would make the journey. My sweet home became a cocoon that fed my senses of smell, touch, hearing and sight of my parents' presence in their absence.

The week before I left home, three years later to join my parents, I walked around the house taking pictures with my mind's eye. I touched the peach-colored walls of my bedroom trailing my fingers between the grooves of the cement blocks. I stood in the corner where I recorded my growth. The fading charcoal bars went from very light to dark rising from the bottom of the wall to where I stood at five-foot-ten.

I knew all the nooks and crannies of that house. I had hidden under my grandmother's bed, behind the metal trunks where she kept the "good" linens and our "good" clothes for special occasions. My siblings and many cousins were always scared to come looking for me, the trunks looked like coffins. I spread the rumors that Grandpa was in one of them, so I was never found when we played hide and seek. I won every time.

The afternoon before my departure, I sat under the mango tree in our backyard next to Grandma as she mended clothes. I gave up on reading when the words swam in my unshed tears. I placed the book on the packed-dirt ground and swallowed the sobs, wishing I could shove them down until they escaped from my bare toes. I hiccupped instead. Grandma lowered her gnarled hands with the crooked needle to her lap and took mine.

"It'll be okay, *pitit mwen,*" she said, kissing my forehead. "You'll be with your Papa and Maman soon."

"But . . . but I don't want to leave you, my friends, my school, my home." I sobbed. "I'm scared, Grandma."

She gathered me in her arms and sang to me like she did when I woke up from a nightmare and crawled in her bed. I never went to my parents' room. Grandma was my anchor. With her around I felt safe, loved, cared for and nothing could harm me.

"Hush, Child. Nothing to be scared about," she whispered.

"I promise to return as soon as I complete my studies and make a lot of money."

"I know, Baby. I'll be here waiting for you," she replied with that all-knowing smile of the wise.

"I'll come back and paint the house bright yellow like the sun. Maybe I'll make it bigger so you can have a room to yourself," I said, feeling hopeful about my plan. "You can put all the good stuffs from under your bed on display. Would you like that, Grandma?" I asked, staring into her weathered and kind face.

"Yes." She nodded. "That'll be real nice. Now you have to go to bed. We're leaving early tomorrow for the airport."

I quietly climbed onto her bed that night and slept in her arms already dreaming of the day I would return home. She gave me a cup of coffee before we boarded the van for the airport. I closed my eyes and held it in my mouth, imprinting the sweet taste to my brain.

I threw myself into my new life in America. My family settled into a grey tenement building in Massachusetts that provided shelter from the elements. It was never a home without Grandma. Our three-bedroom apartment was on the second floor with iron grills on the windows. I wondered at times if the bars were to keep us in or keep danger out. Our neighbors were shadows that darted in and out of their units, avoiding all kind of interaction with their fellow "inmates."

My homesickness became a physical presence that spurred me on to work on my dream of returning home. Then, Grandma joined us, bringing part of our home with her. I graduated from college, got married and started a family. Thus, began my journey of building my own home in America.

Years later, I learned that my beloved home and the whole community in Haiti were torn down by developers. Then in 2009 I boarded that flight to Port-Au-Prince eager to find the home I assumed had replaced my old one and meet the happy family that lived there. I was not prepared for what I found.

The weedy, overgrown, treeless scene that replaced my close-knit, lush and shady neighborhood assaulted my senses. I stood in the middle of the ghost town and heard the protests of the voiceless, marginalized people who were displaced. When my legs could no longer hold the weight of my anger, I knelt and grabbed a fistful of brown dry dirt and sobbed, while screaming, "Why? Why?"

I wept for the majestic almond tree with the hammock that was my favorite place to read. For the families uprooted by greed and tossed about like yesterday's trash at the whims of people with pockets full of cash and fantasy. People, who destroyed homes and lives, then changed their minds like changing their shoes because they didn't match their outfits. I mourned my childhood home and all the wonderful memories that bulldozers could not erase. The small stone in the bottom of my suitcase was all I carried back from my old home to my new one in America.

Maureen Jenkins

# The Fork in the Road

Came that year on a summer day
surrounded by dandelions
and honeysuckle.
                    In my early twenties
with few cares I was tightrope
walking and my self was a la mode
as photographs, monuments,
and memories of childhood days
crumpled, I was eager to travel forward
with my cheap yellow suitcase,
unsure which way to go
as I looked as far as I could,
The road bent and turned and
the grass was green and long.

But now in a flash this summer
evening many years later as
the lightning zigzags across the sky
and the rain crashes on the rooftop,
                    I stand in dark shadows
of the doorway, count down thunder claps
and wonder in this flying moment of time
if I had taken the right fork in the road.

# He Didn't Hit Me

*He didn't hit me*
But he collected my infractions
And lined them up on his desk like surgical knives,
Ready to make another incision
Into the little self-worth I had remaining.
*He didn't hit me*
But when I refused sex,
He would grab my wrists tightly
Until they tingled of needles,
then went numb
And said that if I really loved him,
I would never say no.
*He didn't hit me*
But he went through my phone while I was in the shower
And deleted every contact that was male.
I was a slut.
A whore.
A cunt.
Because I had those numbers in my phone.
If I was to be a good girlfriend,
I could not speak to the opposite sex.
*He didn't hit me*
But he would follow me home
And would show up to my work
To make sure I was not lying about where I was going.
*He didn't hit me*
But I was not allowed to wear makeup
Because that meant I desired the attention of other men.
And once, when I was brave enough
To brush some lipgloss on,
He punched a hole into his bedroom wall,

Right next to my head
And made me wipe it off.
*He didn't hit me*
But the blood in his veins would turn black when he screamed
And I would curl up on the bathroom floor
Sobbing and cowering beneath him
While his hot saliva
Showered onto me.
*He didn't hit me*
But when I threatened to leave
He would send a picture of a knife pressed against his throat
Almost piercing his waning skin,
Promising that he would take his own life
And it would be my fault.
*He didn't hit me*
My wounds were not visible,
But I still have bruises
That will never go away.
*He didn't hit me*
But I become a shell,
And begin to tremble
Every time I hear someone raise their voice.
*He didn't hit me*
But I have dreams that he did.
and in those dreams there is blood,
Broken bones,
And bruises.
In my dreams,
There is proof.
So
Much
Fucking
Proof.

# Robin O'Dell

# Pine Island

The tide is coming in. I haven't been to the beach in many years. I wasn't ready for the rush of visceral memory the waves, sand, smells, and sounds evoked. The salty air sticks to my skin. I fall asleep to the sound of the pounding surf and wake up to the shrieking gulls. We eat shrimp and oysters, drink cold beer, and walk for miles along the beach. This isn't a beach like Pine Island.

Tonight, though, feels like a Pine Island night. It's something in the air, something in the light as the sun slipped down below the horizon. Jim went out fishing all day with friends, and he's dead to the world, asleep on the couch. His sleeping face makes me smile. I'm restless. I take my wine out on the beach and sit in the sand. Tonight I'll let myself remember.

I listen to the crashing waves and imagine I can hear them sighing her name. *Leta, Leta, Leta . . .*

As you get older, you realize that years, days, months—they don't pass the same. What happened ten years ago can feel closer than what happened to you last week.

Twenty years ago I went to Pine Island to escape. I left a family that belittled and humiliated me, a boyfriend who liked to put his hands around my neck and squeeze until I begged him to stop with the breath I had left, and winters that chilled me down to the marrow of my bones. I ended up in Pine Island because the marshes sang a song to my soul that I couldn't ignore. I lived in a one-bedroom house on stilts with a wraparound deck where I could look at the marshes all day. I got a job at the Driftwood Inn, waiting tables. That's where I met Leta.

She'd worked at the Driftwood for a few years. I didn't know anything about waiting tables. Leta didn't really seem to, either, but she told me a lot about the people I'd be working with. We liked to sneak cigarettes and feed the gators off the back deck. She was older than me, everyone was older than me then, with masses of dark wavy hair and amber eyes that could appear almost yellow and looked right through you. Her skin was the prettiest shade of brown, and I always admired her thin brown wrists as they poked out of the white dress shirt we wore to wait tables.

# ODET

We were slammed one Friday night, and I struggled to catch my breath. Back in the kitchen, I watched the servers whirl, faces lined in concentration. Leta was sweating—short with me, no time for chatter. I brought the wrong dish to my table, and the male half of the couple berated me. He'd talk to the manager—have my job! I retreated to the girls' room to cry. Alicia breezed through.

"What's your problem?" she asked, reapplying pink lipstick that didn't need reapplying. (Alicia: two kids, used to be a Weeki Wachee mermaid, drinks too much.)

"I'm having trouble keeping up," I said, trying to stop crying.

"Well, buckle up, Buttercup. The night is young." She gave me a disdainful once-over and left the bathroom. Mermaids don't have time for bullshit.

The door swung open, and Kara barged in. She was already undoing her pants. (Kara: four kids, alcoholic out-of-work husband, works too hard, drinks way too much.) "Outta my way, Penny. I gotta drain the lizard, and I got six tables wondering where I am."

She brushed by me, then saw my tears. "What's wrong with you?"

"I don't think I can do this," I said. Sniveled really. I was the worst.

"Honey." Kara gave me a hug. "It's just work. We'll be done soon, having beers, and talking about how stupid they all are in no time. Just get back out there and get it done."

I washed my face and finished my shift.

Later that night we all drank beer, and we did talk about how stupid the clientele was, and we laughed.

I had too many beers, and Leta walked me home. She came in with me, and we sat at the rickety kitchen table. She fixed me with those eyes of hers, and I found myself talking, talking, talking. I told Leta things I've never told anyone. Hopes, little dreams, disappointments. I told her about my family—my angry father, my spiteful and domineering mother, the brother who used to lock me in the hall closet until I cried. The sordid saga of my loser boyfriend tumbled from my lips.

Leta listened to me; she asked questions. When I started to cry—big, ugly sobs that shook my body—she stood up and held out her hand. She led me to my bedroom, opened a window to let the night sounds in, and helped me into bed. I couldn't stop crying, and Leta quietly slipped into my bed and began stroking my hair. She made soothing sounds, almost like a little song, and I felt a deep sense of peace as my sobs subsided and I drifted to sleep.

When I woke up the next morning, she was gone. I was alone and hungover, and I felt so ashamed of my carrying on the night before.

I left for my shift at the Driftwood later, out of sorts and embarrassed. I didn't know what I would say to her. Leta took one look at me and got up with her arms open wide.

"There she is!" she cried. "My hero." She gave me a warm hug. "You should have seen this one last night," she told the girls. "She drank me under the table, then let me crash at her place to sleep it off. I owe you one," she said to me, giving my arm a squeeze and sitting back down.

Leta was like that. She gave, she listened, and she helped. We were so often together after that night. We drank after shifts together, went for walks along the edges of the marsh, watched sunsets from our favorite spot on Pine Island's small beach. We watched bad TV on my lumpy couch. We exchanged beloved books, so excited to discover the other hadn't yet read this one or that. One cool, windy night, we pulled my mattress out to the porch. We shared a bottle of wine and listened to the marsh. Sometime in the night, there came the mournful sound of a faraway owl, and Leta grabbed my hand. I pretended like I was asleep, and we held hands until the early-morning sun crept onto the porch.

I was becoming a different person, more confident, easy with myself, calmer and centered. I felt smart, interesting. I felt like I was worth something.

Leta was married. His name was Eddie. She rarely spoke of him. He'd show up now and then at the Driftwood. He worked nights and slept days. From what the girls said, he was quiet, kept to himself. When he did show up, he would stare at Leta. Follow her everywhere she went with his dark, hooded eyes.

The first night that changed everything was in September. Thunderstorms made Leta restless, and that month was full of them. She was tense, and we didn't spend as much time together. Dark circles appeared under her eyes, and one night when she was changing out of her work shirt, I saw an ugly pattern of bruises under her arm.

"Are you all right?" I asked.

She froze, then slowly pulled her long-sleeved T-shirt over her head. "Don't worry about me, Penny."

"You know you can tell me if something—"

"I don't want to talk about it, okay?" She grabbed her bag and left.

"You think he's hitting her?" Alicia asked from the doorway.

"I don't know. Do you?" I turned to her.

"What do I know? She's *your* girlfriend." Alicia bumped me with her elbow, then picked her purse up off the table.

"Oh, shut up, Alicia." Face burning, I grabbed my stuff and went out after Leta, but she was already gone.

The next night, Leta didn't show up for her shift. The manager was concerned. "That's not like her. She's not one to pull this kind of crap." She rearranged our sections and yanked on an apron. "I'll take some tables. Did you try calling her, Penny?"

I had. No answer.

We were busy, and it wasn't until after midnight that I had changed into my street clothes. "I'm going to Leta's. This doesn't feel right." I wanted to say it out loud.

Kara nodded. "Let us know what's going on," she said as I left.

As a storm gathered strength, I made my way to Leta and Eddie's cottage. The lights were on.

"Leta?" I called, knocking on the door. "It's Penny. Everything okay?"

The door swung open, and Eddie stood there, glaring at me. "What do *you* want?"

"Leta didn't show for her shift. I just want to check on her." I stood up taller, trying not to be intimidated by his size and anger.

"She's fine. Leave us alone." He started to close the door, but I pushed against it.

"Leta? Are you all right?" I yelled.

"Get out of here," he growled. A bright flash of lightning and deafening boom of thunder made us both freeze. I took advantage of his surprise and muscled past him.

"Leta?" I cried, hurrying through the house.

"Penny."

I stopped, unsure what to do. Leta stood in the middle of the living room. Her eyes were wild, her hair a disheveled mess. "He won't tell me where it is, Penny, and I need to know. I can't stay here any longer. I need to go home." Her voice was strained, her eyes darted around the room.

"Where what is?"

"I can't . . . I can't say, Penny, but I need it. I need to find it." She lunged at me, grasping both of my hands. "Help me, please. Please, Penny, help me.

"I told you to leave," Eddie spat from behind me. Another thunderous crash, and the lights flickered.

"Give her what she wants, and we'll both leave," I said. He was just like my father, blustering and trying to intimidate everyone. "What is it?"

"You don't know what you're talking about," he said, stalking toward us.

I put myself between them. "Then you better tell me."

He raised his hand, and I stared him right in the eyes. I wasn't afraid of him. I wouldn't let him hurt us. "Don't you touch me," I said, a steely reserve in my voice.

He faltered; then a determined look took over his face, and he narrowed his eyes. "You don't know what you're dealing with here. Time to go." He grabbed my arm and yanked me away from Leta, pulled me toward the door.

"Penny!" Leta cried.

There was a blinding flash, and then a whooshing noise that filled the air and made the skin on the back of my neck prickle. The whoosh crackled and grew, and the wall behind us, the wall with the stone fireplace, disappeared with a sickening sound as the thick limb of a tree crashed through it.

The three of us stood in a stupefied daze. Rain poured in from the hole the limb had torn in the ceiling. There were branches and leaves and stone and wood scattered in a crazy jumble. In its midst sat a metal box. Eddie saw it first, and he moved quickly toward it. I saw his face, and I knew—I *knew*—this was what Leta needed. I beat him there and grabbed the box.

"Don't—don't!" I heard him say it even as I popped the lid open.

All I could see were feathers. A box full of brown-and-gold feathers. I looked up at Leta. Her face had transformed. Luminous light shone from her eyes as she came to me and plunged her hands into the box. "Thank you," she whispered, leaning her forehead against mine. "Thank you."

I can't explain what happened next. Leta was there and then she wasn't. In the flickering lights and rain and confusion, I saw her . . . change. An impression of a woman, and then an owl. I blinked, and the owl was gone. I ran outside, and I could see the owl's silhouette, up and up and up, over the trees next to the house, and out of sight.

"You'll never understand what you've done," Eddie snarled. Shoving past me, he ran into the marsh after the owl, disappearing into the night.

I left the island a couple of months later, and I never went back. I heard Eddie stayed, lives there still. Nobody heard from Leta again. I think about what her friendship and her interest and her attention meant, how she helped me, how she buoyed me up and made me see I wasn't worthless. How that time made me who I am today. I think about her impossible amber eyes. On nights like these—these Pine Island nights—I can't get Leta off my mind.

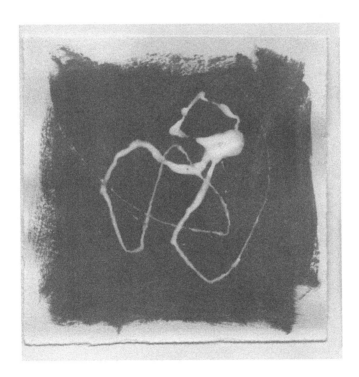

# I Am

*Why are there trees I never walk under but large and melodious thoughts descend upon me?* — *Walt Whitman*

My hair is marsh grass
arms tree limbs
      stretching, muscular in youth
      lowering, frail in old age.

My heartbeat is a frog's
eyes, a bird's
lungs, a fish's
skin, a seal's
      in youth
rough wood bark
      in old age.

My veins line a leaf
blood, a river inside the leaf
breath, is wind a breeze, a gale
the soles of my feet, a bear's.

My bones are rocks, elongated minerals, calcifications
      they will be the heaviness
      you will feel in your palm
my ashes
as you scatter me
to seed new life.

Anda Peterson

# Advice From a Live Oak to the Owner of the Mercedes Floating in the Street in Miami

Listen
Yes, you there
in front of your
winter home in Florida.

Salt water covers
your circular driveway
as you stare with disbelief
at your Mercedes
floating down the street.

Nearby, as if in a dream, you recall words like
carbon footprint, ecosystem
but you don't understand
language not spoken in banks.
You shout
Fix it! Fix it!

You shiver in the heat under the roof
you constructed over the planet.
You shield your eyes
from the harsh landscape
baffled by your own handiwork.

Listen
This is how you got here:
When you cut me and my sap ran
like your own blood
you did not believe we shared in common
the atoms and minerals of the ancient stars died to birth us.
So, I knew that our reunion would have to wait
until we had no choice.
Like now.
I could see
that you were too busy.
You had to conduct a war against all that stood
in your way.
You dug mines, drained swamps, smothered the soil with cement
slashed the forests and fields
forced water where it did not want to flow.

You ordered the seawalls to be rebuilt higher
again and again,
yet the waves roar at them and they succumb
over and over.
Your hand shakes
you grab at your pockets for your rosary of coins.

Now you watch the news and see
Coyotes leap over the walls of guarded houses.
Panthers roam the yards.
Black bears rummage through your trash
swim at their leisure in your Olympic-sized pools.
You have homes hidden behind steel gates
but the animals know these woods and marshes
they have mapped the paths in their veins
feel the contours of the land in their hearts
see through the dark
and know exactly what needs knowing upon the air.

## ODET

For the first time, you hear the alarms.
Your senses open like a deer who listens for the hunter's next step.
The weapon you wielded
has turned on you.
You mowed when it was time to sow.
Demolished what it was time to save.
You understood how to ravage
but not how to prune.

Listen to the plea
in the air all around us
Live
live
live . . .

*Rites of Spring*, Jarine Dotson

# *Hello Kitty* Motorcycle Girl

She's going to kill herself, I thought, as I watched a motorcyclist weave in and out of traffic. My chest tightened. The rider wore hot pink sneakers and a *Hello Kitty* helmet. It had to be a woman. And young. No one over forty would drive so foolishly.

Seconds later, all movement on I-275 stopped. A crumpled bike lay across the left lane, its rider sprawled on the asphalt.

I'd been tracking the rider for over a minute as she'd threaded her way through late rush-hour traffic. Moments earlier, she'd snaked in front of my bumper. I'd slammed my brakes, relieved I'd not hit her and that the car to my rear hadn't rammed into me.

Once across my lane, *Hello Kitty* had ridden her way up the narrow alley of broken lines between tight, bumper-to-bumper traffic.

Now, several eye blinks later, metal lay in the far left lane, about four car lengths in front of me. Some hapless motorist had taken her down. Had *Hello Kitty* been trying to get over into the far left median? Was *that* where she'd planned to ride?

All three lanes of traffic stopped, but only for a few seconds. First, the far right lane began to move, then my center lane eased forward. I inched ahead, gawking like everyone else at the crashed motorcycle. I watched *Hello Kitty* limp across the stopped traffic, her helmet in hand. She stumbled, almost fell, to a seated position in the median, her back leaning against the thick cement barricade separating north and southbound traffic. Several motorists jumped from their cars and surrounded her.

She's lucky, I thought. She's able to walk away.

My husband would later tell me I should've stopped, stayed until law enforcement arrived. "The driver who hit the girl would have appreciated other witnesses to confirm her erratic driving," he'd said.

I shrugged. "I didn't want to be late for my class. Besides, she got up and walked away. It wasn't a big deal."

★ ★ ★

Motorcycles and I have a long, convoluted history beginning in my teens. My older brother joined the Navy, bought a 500cc Indian, and took off on it at every opportunity. One time he rode the small bike from California to Florida to visit the family. I'd felt a dangerous thrill when he took me for a ride. I remember my parents shrugging, none of us thinking about possible accidents but rather how surprising it was my brother had bought a motorcycle. No one in our small community rode one.

We learned the danger of motorcycles three years later, in 1967, when my brother had an accident while crossing the Sierra Nevada Mountains. An unpredicted early snowstorm arose, and he lost control on the slippery, spiraling descent and crashed into a ravine.

Doctors said my brother effectively gave himself a partial prefrontal lobotomy. Years later, my mom, my dad, and I disagreed on how long he remained in a coma. My mom said three days, my dad three weeks, and I remembered three months. At least we agreed on the three. The crash disfigured my brother's face. The internal damage was more difficult to assess and would take years to fully determine.

Several months later, both the hospital and the Navy discharged my brother, and he came home to recuperate. I was away at school by this time. He didn't stay home long. He found employment despite his injuries, and moved out within a few months. He never replaced his totaled motorcycle, selecting a Karmann Ghia instead. Again, my parents and I looked at his car choice with surprise. We'd never seen or heard of a Karmann Ghia back in 1968. No one in our small town drove such an unusual-looking vehicle.

I never thought much about my brother's injuries, despite all the scars on his face. Nor did I give another thought to the dangers of motorcycles. At nineteen, I was too caught up in my own dramas to care much about anything or anyone else.

★ ★ ★

When *Easy Rider* hit the movie theaters in 1969, my fascination with motorcycles mushroomed. I didn't put the big choppers Peter Fonda and Dennis Hopper rode in the same category as my brother's little 500cc Indian. Plus, there was nothing countercultural whatsoever about my brother. He was just showing off and trying to be different. In contrast, Fonda and Hopper were honest-to-God bad boys and unlike anyone I'd ever known. They made political and philosophical statements with their motorcycles, and they aroused in me a latent longing to shock and offend.

Motorcycling became fixed in my mind not only as a symbol for being bad and nonconforming but for being free. *Easy Rider* embodied all the acting-out rebellion I'd later express as I marched down streets—protesting the war in Vietnam, lobbying for women's rights, and fighting racism. Those late sixties and early seventies were glorious and glamorous years for me, a time when I knew the revolution was around the corner and I was helping to bring it about.

Politics aside, there were times when the image of tooling down the road on a motorcycle, side-by-side with an amigo, passing a doobie back and forth between the bikes for the sheer fun of it, hounded my imagination. I could totally see me doing that.

But I never did.

★ ★ ★

A couple of decades later, around 1986, a Kodak commercial on television rekindled memories of those vicarious *Easy Rider* thrills. I think Kodak was promoting yet another of its many Instamatic cameras. The ad showed a rugged-looking young man riding around the country on a 250cc Honda Rebel motorcycle. Honda had modeled the Rebel after the Harley low-rider, the prototype for the choppers in the movie.

In the television commercial, this macho Kodak-ad hunk stopped his travels at various spots to gaze at snow-covered mountains, to camp beside wooded streams, and to watch sunsets on pristine beaches. Every place he stopped, he'd take out his Instamatic and snap a few pictures.

While I knew Kodak was trying to sell cameras, their commercial sold me on the idea of buying a motorcycle. The Honda Rebel was too adorable and affordable to pass up. Plus, I was in the throes of a major midlife crisis. Before long, I scooted around town on my own little Honda Rebel, buried deep in personal *Easy Rider*/Kodak fantasies. I wanted to break away from restrictive middle-class mores. I wanted to be bad. Riding a motorcycle became synonymous with everything I'd ever wanted but had lacked the courage to do. Maybe, at last, on my Rebel, I could become the rebel I longed to be.

I'm not proud of my two years of acting out with a motorcycle, despite somehow managing to keep my professional employment and not horrifying the parents of my children's friends too much. I considered motorcycle ownership a celebration of the demise of a fourteen-year marriage. It represented an ultimate rejection of all the hoity-toity, academic, ivory-towered self-righteousness my marriage had contained. I was a parent, however, and could only enjoy my liberated persona when my children went to their dad's house. Then I could metamorphose into a huge and wild alter ego, a la Rose in the *Rose is Rose* cartoon strip. In her biker alter ego role,

Rose forgets she's Jimbo's wife and Pasquale's mom as she emerges into a formidably exaggerated biker chick. Most of the time, though, my life continued as before. I chauffeured my kids to piano and dance lessons, Little League practices and games, birthday parties, and G-rated movies. In my Toyota Corolla.

Although my secret life was fun, I look back in horror at some of my escapades. In less than a year, I'd met and fallen in love with a biker, a testosterone-driven man who, in retrospect, was anathema to almost everything I believed in. He was a career Air Force veteran, a fighter pilot who'd served four tours of duty in Vietnam. I cringe now to realize he'd been dropping bombs in Southeast Asia as I screamed anti-war sentiments at rallies in Washington, D.C. He was, however, an icon of wasted brilliance and unused talents, and I'd long been a sucker for underachieving men.

Before long, I upgraded my little Rebel to a 500cc Honda Silverwing. My boyfriend rode a fully dressed 1300cc Honda Goldwing with a sidecar. Not a real biker, obviously, since he rode a Japanese-built bike, but I'd learned this was nothing to joke about. In my boyfriend's mind, he was authentic.

If I'd been thinking during this two-year period as I enacted my own screenplay of *Easy Rider*, I'd have realized riding a bike with a bomb-dropping veteran was not what Fonda and Hopper had been about on their cross-country trip. However, I did have an exciting *Easy Rider*-type experience when the boyfriend and I passed a flask of blackberry brandy back and forth between the bikes on I-275 at four o'clock one morning, in thirty-something degree temperatures going about eighty-five m.p.h. He convinced me the brandy was necessary to stay warm on the thirty-mile trip from my house to his.

I admitted the utter wrongness of this relationship on a cross-country road trip to Sturgis, South Dakota for Bike Week. I won't embarrass myself by sharing the juicy details of all the things that went wrong as my boyfriend and I headed west from Tampa towards Sturgis. I will only say that in Omaha, Nebraska, I made a definitive U-turn in the road. While he continued to ride west, I headed east. I came back home.

The solo ride from Omaha to Tampa on my motorcycle proved to be the most empowering experience of my life. Riding through the Blue Ridge Mountains, I had one of those exhilarating peak feelings that if I went over the side of the mountain and died, it would all have been worth it because I'd die doing exactly what I wanted to do. I savored freedom on this trip home as I'd never tasted it before. My takeaway was that I'd never again let a man control me the way my boyfriend had done.

I sold the bike after getting home from the aborted Sturgis trip and settled back down into a mature, responsible lifestyle. Or at least it appeared that way on the surface. My friends and family expressed relief to have me back and to have the motorcycle sold. In many ways, I was, too. I'd finally gotten that out of my system.

It took a couple more decades of living and maturing to understand, even a tiny bit, the anguish my parents must have felt during the two-year period when I rode a motorcycle. Their son lived with permanent brain damage from a motorcycle accident, and now their daughter flirted with a similar fate. My parents' nightmares must have been terrifying, their cold sweats drenching, their near heart attacks excruciating. When the subject of my motorcycle arose, however, they maintained a tight-lipped, stone-cold silence. I'm not sure why.

If my parents were still alive, I'd tell them how sorry I am to have put them through such anxiety with my motorcycle. I'd never try to explain to them why I'd done it, though. I'm not sure they'd have understood why I'd found tempting the gods, playing the odds, and defying death by riding a motorcycle so exhilarating and compelling.

★ ★ ★

About ten years ago, while on vacation, we watched a huge, fully-dressed Honda Goldwing, 1500cc, three-wheeler pull into a parking lot at Mount St. Helens, Washington. A silver-haired couple climbed off.

"Let's go talk to them." With my eyes wide and my jaw dropped, I felt myself drawn to this couple and their bike like a cat to catnip. I had to hear their story.

My reluctant husband followed me across the parking lot. We learned the couple was celebrating retirement with a three-month trip across the country. They were stopping to gaze at snow-covered mountains, camping beside wooded streams, and watching sunsets on pristine beaches. My long-buried *Easy Rider*/Kodak longing roared back to life.

Michael wanted no part of it. Motorcycles scared the bejesus out of him and he made it adamantly clear he'd never, ever, under any circumstances, climb on one to even go to the end of our street and back, let alone across the country. He wanted to travel though, which led him to buy an RV as soon as he retired. He tried to convince me that RV travel would produce the same thrill as riding a motorcycle. Maybe for him.

I didn't try to explain to him how untrue that would be for me. Or how profoundly disappointed I felt to once again have my dream denied.

★ ★ ★

As I picked up speed on I-275, relieved I wouldn't be late for class, all these motorcycle memories flashed through my mind. I'm not over it, I realized. Given a partner who'd ride with me, I'd be down at the Honda dealer this afternoon, ordering my own custom-built, full-dressed Honda Goldwing Trike, 1833cc, six-cylinders and with a 7-speed automatic transmission. I could release my alter ego with a bike like that. I'd probably be safe enough, even with my slowed-down reflexes, poor balance, and arthritic joints. After all, those three-wheelers are almost as big as Volkswagen bugs. With enough flashing vanity lights, drivers would see me. And with three wheels, I wouldn't have to worry about falling over. Surely my deteriorated hands still had enough strength to operate the handlebar controls to accelerate and brake.

The image of *Hello Kitty* weaving in and out of traffic haunts me. I want to hunt her down, shake her until her teeth fall out, and tell her to stop being so damned stupid. I'd explain she's living my dream, but that she's not respecting it. If she understood what she had, she wouldn't mess it up with careless mistakes. I'd say she's smart to do this while she's young, that when she gets old, this dream might not be reachable. I'd beg *Hello Kitty* to swear to her parents she wouldn't crash and end up with her brains oozing out of her nose. And I'd scream in her face that this minor accident on I-275 was a wake-up call, a warning she needed to be more careful with her life.

Finally, I'd tell *Hello Kitty* to keep her girlie footwear and eye-candy headgear. That if I ever mustered the courage to ride again, I'd dress just like her. Surely motorists would watch out for a little seventy-year-old woman on a motorcycle, especially one wearing hot pink sneakers and a *Hello Kitty* helmet.

Karen Koven

# I Climbed into Carl Sandburg's Lap

I climbed into Carl Sandburg's lap. I was 7.
His harvest-moon-white-buster-brown-cut mop of hair
was like nothing I'd ever seen.
Our teacher, with the grace of an industrious sheep dog,
herded us to the reading center's pink chenille carpet.
She guided Sandburg to the front of our cross-legged crescent
where he folded himself into one of the student chairs.

"The fog," he began in his soothing bedtime-story-voice.
"The fog comes in on little cat feet."
I could see the fog. I could feel its approach. I could smell the heavy damp air.
I could not hear it because it was coming in on cat feet. The fog-cat enveloped me.
I strained to hear its unseen paws.

Sandburg's strange and wonderful hair dominated his form.
We were all aching to touch it.
One of the boys pressed Sandburg, "Can I touch your hair?"
The gentle poet leaned forward, like a cat inviting a tender caress.
In an instant, all of us, all 15 or so of us,
climbed and clamored our way to his buster-brown-crown, like a box of puppies.

*Digging a Hole to China*, George Chase

# Rocky Road Runaround

They huddled in the sun shaking, even though it was pushing ninety degrees. The kids had just finished another tubing run down Deep Creek, with its fifty-something degree water. It was their sixth run of the morning. With the creek hidden beneath a full canopy of oaks and myrtles, finding our campsite from the stream was a challenge. They had pinballed among the sun spotted boulders until I waved them ashore. Normally, by this time of the day, I would have been as shriveled up and cold as they were, but I'd recently had back surgery. My job on this trip was to drag the kids ashore before they ended up somewhere down in the next state.

They glanced at me, whispering, and then harmonized, "Can we *please* have some Rocky Road ice cream?"

Ready to do something, anything, I volunteered to drive down to Bryson City.

"You're a good dad," my wife said, not knowing my true motives.

Having paid for the high-performance suspension package on our new Cadillac sedan, I wanted to get a feel for it. The flat roads back home in Florida simply didn't challenge the car's road-hugging potential. Its fat tires crunched over the crushed granite access road, while the essence of spruce, wafting off the mountain, mingled with that new-car smell. With only a hint of tire chirp, I banked through each turn at the maximum legal limit.

*I should run all the way down to Ashville. No, I should get back before the kids get bored and hike back up the mountain for another run. Ice cream won't last long in this heat.*

Chirping into the parking lot, maybe just a little too fast, I parked beside a team of Clydesdales pulling a wagon with a Dalmatian perched on the seat. Sweat dripped from the driver's face as he unloaded two more cases of Budweiser. My car looked pretty slick sitting beside his truck with its mural of trotting horses, so I snapped a picture with my cell phone before walking inside the Piggly Wiggly.

Having never been inside that particular grocery store, I guessed and turned left, searching down each aisle for the freezers. Reaching the far wall, I spotted the deli on the opposite side of the store and realized they normally kept the ice cream near the cakes, which were always near the bakery.

*Why am I always wrong when I have a fifty-fifty chance?*

Completing an entire lap of the store, I arrived back at the checkout counter nearest the door I'd entered. Only two counters were open, one at each end of the store, so I once again had a fifty-fifty chance of picking the slowest line. A woman in bib overalls stepped up as I arrived. She held only a single loaf of bread, so I waved her ahead of me.

"Thank you, sir," she said. "Hurry up, Little Billy," she yelled down the aisle.

As I turned, six-foot-plus Little Billy strolled up, pushing a cart piled high with canned goods and pulling a second, nearly as full.

He nodded. "Thanks buddy."

Knowing my ice cream wouldn't last the duration, I slipped away unnoticed. Trotting to the far end of the store, I waited in the express lane. Two six-packs and a carton of cigarettes later, I stepped out into the blazing sun.

The beer truck was gone, but a flock of RV's had settled upon the lot. "Made it just in time," I mumbled as the teeming horde descended upon the store. Seeing nothing but campers and little beyond, I walked the lot, assuming another full lap would be necessary, but, lo and behold, there it sat. Fishing for my keys, I approached the car, which now seemed to be leaning.

Stepping around to the passenger side, I groaned. "That was a brand-new tire."

The spare was obviously still good, although my back twinged at the thought alone. Searching the storefronts along Highway 19, I spotted a tire store, two blocks down. With a huff, I began walking, Rocky Road in hand.

*Better on my shoes than on the Cadi's new carpet.*

Sweating profusely, I nodded to the man behind the counter. His nametag read Zach.

"Hot enough for you?" Zach asked.

"You know it. Can you fix a flat for me? I've got a bad back. My car's just down the road, out in the parking lot of the Piggly Wiggly."

"What? They wouldn't let you bring it inside?"

I stared at him for a moment, but then he grinned.

"Just pullin' your leg. Fifty minimum for service calls on Saturday."

"How much during the week?"

"Fifty."

"Um . . . okay. That includes patching the tire, right?"

"Yep. Removal, repair, and installation."

"And air?"

"Yes, sir. Air's free. Head on back. I'll meet you up there. My truck's only got the one seat."

I placed the ice cream in the shade of the Cadillac's rear bumper and watched Zack make the repairs. His truck, although a pile of rust, had everything he needed. After jacking up the car, he used an air wrench to remove the wheel. He even had one of those tire machines in the bed, so he rolled the tire off the rim, removed the nail, and patched the hole from the inside.

Ten minutes later, he said, "There you go. That'll be sixty dollars."

"You said fifty."

"Well ain't you gonna tip me?"

Handing him three twenties, I said, "Keep the change." As Zack drove away, I bent down for the Rocky Road under the bumper.

"What ya' doing, mister?"

Turning as I stood, I found myself face to whiskers with Little Billy. "Me?" I said, taking a step back.

The lady in the overalls pointed her key at the trunk—and it popped. She frowned. "What'd you put under my Cadi?"

"Your Cadi?" I said, reaching down for my bag of ice cream. Face high with the back bumper, my eyes found the license plate—the North Carolina license plate.

Little Billy laughed. "You thought this here was your car."

I smiled as I stood with the bag. "I do have one just like it." I turned, scanning the lot. Ten rows over, by the far entrance, I spotted my car. "Way over there. I—I saw yours and wondered if you'd paid for the optional high-performance rear suspension too."

"Livin' in these here mountains? You know we did," Little Billy said. "We ain't stupid."

As I grinned up at him, a dollop of Rocky Road splashed down on the toe of my shoe. "Well . . . I better run. Have a nice day," I said, turning back toward the store. I dropped the leaking bag of *Muddy* Road in the trash as I stepped through the door.

Completing another lap of the store—you'd think my odds would have been better—I arrived back at the original checkout, which by then was the only one open. But my luck had apparently changed, because the counter was clear, the groceries bagged, and the elderly woman was rummaging in her huge purse for her billfold—or so I thought.

"How much did you say?" she asked the clerk.

"Forty-nine thirty-two, ma'am."

"Oh my," the lady said, lifting a Mason jar from her bag. "I sure hope I got enough," she added, dumping pennies onto the counter.

Chuckling, I pulled three twenties from my wallet.

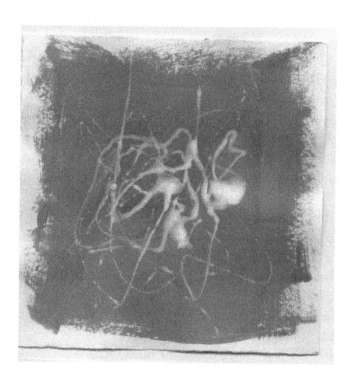

# The Iron Horse

From nine to five, the trail she ran
A solemn monotony
Perhaps along her brethren
Kentucky, and Tennessee

Her job's a rather easy one
"Take the food to random port!"
Certainly not her only trip
She helped storm Indian forts!

She'd guided black slaves, side by side
Escaping for their freedom
And crossed the canyon bridges
And explored the Spanish kingdoms

Sometimes gunfights, sometimes robberies
Never a moment dull
Paving through the wilderness
Catching cow and bull

She visited cities in her work
Mankind's greatest creations
Palaces! Theaters! Barriers!
Glass and iron stations

Many authors passed with her
She'd watch them write, and see
One victim, thirteen murderers
On an Orient mystery

She'd race the winding streams and gullies
Where Conestogas went
But met her match in the city
A man by name of Kent

Her directions? North by Northwest
Her motive? Nothing but steam
'Tween Baltimore and Ohio
A river or a coal seam

Then one day, her employer stopped
And bricked up the old route
"New money!" they said, "New jobs!" they said
And left her, cold, without

She sits there still, dead to the world
As the engines pass her by
As younger women do the work
That once held her so high

But if you walk out near the tracks
Beneath a wilderness sky
The old folks say, if you listen hard
Her thoughts of days gone by

"I paved the way, for pioneers
Where eddying currents swirled
A final whistle, echoing
Conqueror of the Western world!"

# On Cars and Great Explorations

Great Explorations, the St. Petersburg Children's Museum, became my favorite place to take my two-year-old grandson, particularly when it was too hot to go outside but he was too energetic to keep inside. His favorite activity was a large open arena that held hundreds of blue foam blocks, each block almost as tall as he was. On this day, we were in the arena without a remedy; he sat at my feet with only one block in his arms. We both eyed the other blocks. They were stacked up to look like a life-size futuristic automobile, complete with flaps and whirly-gigs.

A young blond boy, maybe 10 years old, had used all of the blocks to build the car. He must have already worn out the patience of the teen volunteer who often stayed in the arena. Usually helpful, when she saw me talking with him, she turned and headed in the other direction.

When the boy noticed us eyeing his car, he misunderstood. I was wondering if I could steal a few blocks for my grandson; he started explaining how the car worked. I began planning how to carry my grandson away without a toddler meltdown. Then the boy said something about how the car was spin-proof and crash-proof. Those words sent me into a tail-spin memory.

I was seventeen and doing exactly what I wasn't supposed to be doing: driving a carload of my friends on an icy, snowy night in Michigan, on an unfamiliar highway, at two in the morning. We were hurrying back from a concert we weren't supposed to be attending. My old green Plymouth had a push button transmission and bald tires. It didn't matter that I had little on-the-road diving experience, and had missed regular driver's training because I waited tables all summer to buy the car. I worked. I owned a car. My four friends expected me to drive. They each chipped in a dollar for gas.

We were hurrying because the concert, about two hours north of our homes in Flint, Michigan, lasted far past our curfews. *Question Mark and the Mysterians* played nothing but variations on *96 Tears* over and over, but we stayed until the very end. As we raced home it began to rain, then the rain turned to ice, followed by blowing snow.

I didn't see the curve until I was in it, heading straight at 60 mph, while the road turned sharply to the left. When I hit the brakes and turned the steering wheel, the car began to spin. I remembered to pump the brakes and steer into the curve, as written in my driver's training manual, but the car ignored me and continued to spin.

We began to donut through the countryside across the two lanes of highway. I saw a huge oak tree on the other side of the road directly in our path. I knew we would hit it at an awful speed, and there was nothing I could do. The car wasn't responding.

But here's where things got weird. My body wanted to brace for the impact, but instead, everything slowed down. Just like the cliché. Time slowed down. As though I were watching a home movie, I saw my life. First, images from infancy. It felt like I was recalling them for the first time, but I recognized them. Next, my early childhood played out in front of me. Then, scenes from my later childhood and early teens. I saw conversations that had taken place, events, scenes, people. Everything, seemingly every moment, came back to me in order. As each scenario unfolded, it was as though a question was being posed to me. Had I done the right thing?

One particular scenario came out of nowhere. When I was 15, a group of us were at the Dairy Queen, eating soft serve cones. A young blond boy, maybe 10, attached himself to our group and started talking to me. We were looking at the stars and began to talk about the constellations. I was a weird, geeky kid, and astronomy had recently gotten me excited. We talked for a while until I noticed my cousins whispering and pointing at us. I turned my back on him and blew him off.

I swear I never had a second thought about that event. But on that night, spinning across the highway, I realized it hurt him. He needed someone to talk to, someone interested in the things he cared about. I could have been that someone. Had I done the right thing? *Had I been helpful?* the voice in my head asked me.

As my memories caught up in time and space with the spinning vehicle, I again saw the huge oak tree coming straight at me, getting larger and larger in the windshield, inevitable. I will never forget when my front bumper made contact with that tree.

I composed myself enough to step out of the car and look. It appeared the front bumper kissed the tree. No crash, no damage; a soft stop, the car gently touching the base of the big oak. Everyone was out of the car hugging each other; they began pounding my back, congratulating me for being a great driver. I'd done nothing other than endangering them in the first place. I never regained control of the steering. When we finally drove away, I left thinking not about the almost-crash, or even about my whole-life-review, but about the questions that came with it.

My grandson pulled at my leg and I realized I was standing in a museum in St. Petersburg, Florida, next to a young boy describing his car of the future. I wanted to get away from him; I was here to pay attention to my grandson. But I remembered that very similar boy up north: intelligent, quirky, and oblivious to most social cues. Needing attention.

So, I let him tell me about his car; how he designed it and why it couldn't crash. My grandson even appeared to listen. I asked him questions, explained what ideas I thought were solid, and told him people of the future would find this car amazing. He put his hands in his pockets, rocked back on his heels, and smiled.

I have done no research about the life-flashing-before-your-eyes or time-slowing-down phenomena. I can't say if it's a function of the brain, a religious experience, or entirely in one's imagination. I only know it happened to me. And, in the end, I am responsible for the good I create in life; whether I have done the right things and said the little things that might make a difference in the lives of others.

And who knows? Maybe that boy's car design will one day save the lives of some other teens, hurrying to get from one place to another in the middle of the night.

# Our Perspective: Part 2

He asked for identification. I reached for my identification.
The police yelled, "There's a gun! Shoot!"
He followed the command.
The officers knew it was a wallet.
I'm pretty sure he said he felt threatened.

Or was it because I am black?

Can you please tell me this: Why haven't we gotten a state writing prompt on the justice system? I'm not talking about informative. We need an argumentative piece. They need to hear our voice.

Innocent black people killed or beaten over a wallet they asked for. Using their own words against them.

"I need identification."

We proceed to pull out our wallet, scared any movement will make them think we have a gun. It can be a boy or a girl. We are tired of seeing our people leaving this world just because of our skin color.

There is no "land of the free." ARE WE PRIVILEGED enough to be treated right?
Our justice system is broken.

# Breathe the Sea

Jeremy's bare feet pounded on the forest floor as he ran. "Come on, Mason, keep up!" he called over his shoulder. "The pirates are gaining on us."

"I'm right here." Mason's sword reflected the sunlight that shone through the trees as he jerked to a stop.

Jeremy stopped, too. "What is it?" he asked. Mason put a finger to his lips. They listened. Leaves crunched on the ground nearby. Then the small clearing swarmed with pirates.

"Attack!" Jeremy yelled. Swords clashed as he and Mason fought them off until the pirates, overwhelmed by their skill, retreated into the woods.

"They're going to get the gold," Mason cried.

"We have to stop them." Jeremy took a step.

"Jeremy!"

"Yeah?" He turned, but Mason was gone.

The forest was silent, apart from his mother's voice. "Jeremy! Time for dinner!"

Jeremy dragged his feet as he headed back toward the house. His shoulders drooped now that Mason was gone. Mason was his best friend. *His only friend.* As Mason always liked to point out.

Back at the house, Jeremy's mother looked up from her laptop at the kitchen table. "Look how dirty you are. You're ten years old. You shouldn't be running around the woods, by yourself, barefoot."

"Mason was with me."

She sighed. "You know there aren't any kids around here called Mason. Have you gotten *any* homework done today?"

"I don't like sitting at the computer for so long. It hurts my eyes."

"No, it doesn't. Get yourself cleaned up, it's time for di—" Her cellphone rang. She picked it up and went to her office.

Jeremy walked through the living room. Lights flashed from the TV screen as his two sisters played some sort of game. Anna, a year younger than him, wore a virtual reality headset. Britt, two years older than Jeremy, unfortunately noticed him.

"Hey, Freak. Have fun with your imaginary friends?"

Jeremy tried to ignore her.

"Are you mute, now, Dumbo?" Anna chimed in. "You're so stupid, you don't even know how stupid you are."

"Come play a real game. Oops, I forgot. You're so out of tune with life, you don't even know what a TV is."

"Yeah. Do you, like, even know where you are right now?"

"Wait, where you goin'? Freak."

They laughed as he climbed the stairs. Tears spilled from his eyes. He never came back down for dinner.

Two months later, on a vacation to Florida, the family fell into a routine. They would all go to the beach outside their hotel where Britt and Anna would play in the sand, building intricate sandcastles. Jeremy's mother would sit in the shade of an umbrella, updating her social media pages. His father would sit tanning in the sun, tablet in hand.

And Jeremy would swim. Constantly, constantly swim.

One beautiful morning, he was especially enjoying himself, free of the stress of his family, even if it was only temporarily. He dove into the turquoise with a bubbly splash, Mason not far behind.

They leaped through the rolling waves, and chased schools of shimmering silver fish into patches of seagrass. Mason discovered a huge lightning whelk, bigger than both his hands combined, then Jeremy came across little seahorses clinging to strands of seagrass.

A shadow of movement caught Jeremy's eye.

A sea turtle!

Jeremy swam with the sea turtle, mimicking the way she flapped her front fins, gliding through the water. Mason left, but Jeremy didn't really care.

He followed the turtle farther and farther out. The water turned from shallow with a warm, yellow light rippling on the swaying sea grass to deeper water with gradient shades of blue. The sunbeams piercing the water struggled to reach the sand below. Shadows loomed ahead.

*Rocks*, Jeremy thought.

But as he swam closer, he realized the shadows weren't just rocks, but also pieces of a sunken ship.

In awe, he abandoned his tail on the sea turtle and swam closer to inspect the wreck.

The thick wooden planks were scattered about. Rotting, with algae and coral taking over, there wasn't much left of the ship. Unfazed by the "disappointment" of the ship's remains, Jeremy explored and discovered a gaping black hole. It went straight into the earth.

Excited, Jeremy began to swim down. Only a little ways in, he felt the water stir beside him.

He froze. It was something big. *Mason?* He wasn't sure.

Not able to see even his hand in front of his face, he was regretting his decision to swim into the deep, dark hole.

Something grabbed his arm and yanked him back up into the blue. It couldn't be Mason, his imagination wasn't that strong. Jeremy yelped and squeezed his eyes shut, not wanting to see the creature about to eat him.

Then something soft stroked his cheek.

Jeremy cracked an eye open and gasped. It wasn't Mason or a terrifying monster, but a girl. She looked to be around Britt's age and stared at him with large eyes, nearly twice the size of his. The pupil filled the majority of the eye, but a thin sparkle of green lined the black before reaching a small amount of white.

A mixture of curiosity, annoyance, concern, and fear shone on her heart-shaped face. Her long, long white hair and shell-white skin gave her a ghostly appearance. She wore nothing over her upper-body, and her pale belly merged into blue-green scales. Jeremy gaped at the long, slender tail that gracefully swept back and forth.

His jaw dropped. He was looking at *a mermaid.*

He dared to brush the girl's cheek with the back of his fingertips, the way she had done to him. She flinched slightly, but didn't break eye contact.

A *real* mermaid.

A series of clicks and whistles came from the mermaid's moving mouth. It sounded like a whale call, but different. It echoed in Jeremy's head as though that's where he was hearing it.

The mermaid stopped whistling and looked at Jeremy hopefully. He shook his head, his mouth still hanging open. He couldn't understand her.

She bit her lip and glanced behind nervously. Such a familiar and human-like gesture coming from such a foreign, yet human-like creature made Jeremy wonder. Really, how different were they?

*You should not go down hole. Angry octopus lives in hole.*

Jeremy startled at the voice in his head. It was soft, foreign, and musical. *Beautiful,* he thought.

*Many thanks.* Her voice was in his head.

*You can hear my thoughts?* Jeremy asked in his mind.

*Thoughts?* She squinted in confusion. *You speak. I hear you speak. I answer.*

*That's so cool! How do you know English?*

*English?* She shook her head. *We speak water.*

*Awesome!*

She smiled.

*My name's Jeremy. Do you have a name?* he asked.

*Not in Human. Only in Sea.* She squeaked a sequence of chirps.

*I don't think I can pronounce that.* Jeremy gazed at the beautiful creature before him. With her pale skin and hair, and tail that matched the blues of the sea, she almost looked to be invisible. See-through . . . *Sheer,* Jeremy thought. *Oops, sorry. I didn't mean to say that, um, out loud.*

*Sheer,* the mermaid repeated. *Pretty.*

*You like that?*

She nodded.

*Would it be okay to call you Sheer?*

She nodded again. *And I call you Sand. Like the color of your hair.*

*But I already have a name.*

*So do I,* Sheer said, a challenge in her voice.

*Okay. That's true.* Jeremy chuckled. *Sand is good. I like that.*

Sheer's smile grew wider. *I watch you swim.*

You did? *Why?*

*You don't take breaths. Not one. You breathe the sea. Like me.*

Jeremy stared. Could it be true? He hadn't even noticed that he had not gone up for air. He had been having too much fun. *You think I'm a mermaid? I mean, merman—obviously.* He puffed out his chest.

Sheer shook her head with a smile. *Mermaid . . . merman? No, Sea People.*

*But, Sheer . . . I was born in Michigan. Miles from the ocean. I don't have a tail!*

Sheer looked at his legs, humor in her eyes. *True. Clumsy legs.*

Jeremy looked at his legs and laughed. Then he sobered, his thoughts turning to his unhappy life away from the sea. *Seriously, though. It sounds crazy, but can I somehow get a tail?* It would be such an adventure traveling the endless ocean together.

Sheer cocked her head. *I will ask elders.*

*Wait-what? There are more mer—uh, Sea People?*

*Yes, Sea People family. Ocean life, too. All family. All one.*

*But how do you know I'm part of it all?* Jeremy asked, hoping it might be possible.

*You speak water. You breathe the sea. You family.*

A smile grew on Jeremy's face. Sheer grinned back. They spent the rest of the day swimming around the rocks and coral, playing tag and hide-and-go-seek. A dolphin appeared and joined their games.

Then, out of nowhere, came a deafening roar. A boat slowed at the surface. The dolphin disappeared as divers jumped into the water. Radio static bounced back and forth between them.

Sheer swam into the octopus hole with a lighting fast flick of her tail. Jeremy swam after her, but much slower due to his "clumsy legs." Sheer pulled him down next to her.

*Too late, Sand. They spot you.* He could barely make out her pale, pretty face in the darkness. Anger bloomed in his chest. He knew his parents were behind the boat and the divers. They wanted to steal him back.

*I don't want to go. I belong with you,* Jeremy said.

*You stay in here, they steal me, too.* Her voice broke in his head.

Jeremy puffed out his chest. He had seen enough mermaid movies to know he *couldn't* let the humans find Sheer. His chest deflated. *But I don't want to leave.*

*You must. For now.* Sheer put her hands on his shoulders. *Come back.* She pecked his lips, then pushed him out of the hole.

The divers reached Jeremy and grabbed him. As they swam to the surface, Jeremy didn't tear his gaze away from the thin, sparkling green circles that stared up from the darkness.

*I'll come back, Sheer. To you and the sea. I promise.*

Jeremy was taken to the hospital where his parents were waiting. He tried to convince them that he had to go back to the ocean. "Why?" they asked. At first, he didn't answer. But eventually, his frustration led to him admitting he had to go back to his mermaid-friend, Sheer, so that he could breathe the sea and join the ocean family.

Saying that was a grave mistake. He was taken to doctors, therapists, specialists . . . none of them "worked." He still insisted he needed to get back to the ocean.

Jeremy had been in and out of many mental institutes by the time he was seventeen. His parents rarely visited him during those stays, and when they did, they couldn't even look at him.

Jeremy was alone.

★ ★ ★

He slowly opens his eyes. The ocean far below is blue and sparkling, it reflects the endless sky above.

He's so high up, seagulls fly below him. The wind blows cool and strong. Cars race by just behind him, but no one stops for the sad man on the bridge's edge, yearning to join the ocean life.

He leans over the railing. The sea beckons, yet he hesitates.

*They say she's fake, a figment of my imagination. They're getting in my head. I'm starting to believe them. I can't—*

"Why can't you believe them, Jeremy?" Mason dangles his legs over the rail a few feet away. "Why can't you accept the fact that you're a lunatic?"

Jeremy shuts his eyes and breathes a lungful of salty air.

"Go away, Mason. You and I both know you're fake."

"How do you know Sheer isn't fake, too?"

Jeremy shakes his head. *Is he right? Am I actually insane? Did I dream her up? Have I been delusional my entire life?*

He leans farther over the railing. *So close . . .* "Goodbye, Mason."

"What?"

Jeremy stares hard at Mason. Mason glares back.

"I know she's real." Jeremy lifts himself until he's crouched, balanced on the rail. He looks down. His heart beats wildly at the dizzying drop. *She's real.*

He jumps.

He falls.

His heart flies.

He hasn't felt this free in twenty-three years.

*I'm coming, Sheer, just as I promised.*

The wind roars in his ears. Tears blur his vision. The sparkling blue grows larger and larger, until it's so large, it swallows him whole.

# The Wind, on Being Free

I don't worry about my direction—
my path could go anywhere.
My temperature is immaterial.

What matters is my volume: I give everything I have.

I adore bringing out the voices of others, the soft-voiced ones.
I whisper, and sometimes I howl.
I carry distant sound, or obliterate everything with my roar.
I caress you or I bowl you over in my enthusiasm.
I am the voice of life, rains, spring, seeds, renewal.
I am the voice of destruction—
I rearrange the oceans and the land.
I carry life, and I carry death:
all things are equal to me.

I am the creator of dance and motion,
and I know how to stand aside for stillness.

I am the movement of the spirit: free and kind and without limit.
Giving, giving, giving.

*Beauty Lies in the Broken Path*, Terrie Dahl Thomas

*The History of Point A to Point B*, Terrie Dahl Thomas

# Six States, Ten Houses

the sound of packing tape ripping
like a clap of thunder on a sunny day,
the lingering smell of bad breath and smoked cigarettes,
and i can't tell if it's my bedroom or
the gas station around the corner.

six states, ten houses
eating cold leftover pizza on the dirty tile
listening to the echoes of the empty house,
wondering if it will whisper our secrets
to the next family.

six states, ten houses
the neon orange moving stickers
appear all over my body like hives
and by the time i remove them
more appear, but this time they're
neon green.

six states, ten houses
same mental asylum white interior paint
same desert tan exterior paint that
matches every other house in the neighborhood.

six states, ten houses
what's it like to know where the
mugs are kept in the cupboard?
to open the first drawer and actually
find the spoons?

# ODET

six states, ten houses
four therapists.

six states, ten houses
i keep an old photo of my dad under my pillow
from when he still had a 90s high fade haircut
my grandma wrote our names on the back of the photo
but the ink has started to smudge from
years of tears from trips and deployments.

six states, ten houses
running to hold onto the fragile ceramics
every time a thunder jet broke
the sound barrier over our roof.

six states, ten houses
if you sliced my veins open,
red, white, blue,
and faded green camo
would unwillingly come spilling out.

six states, ten houses
after a nomadic life,
how am i suddenly supposed to
know how to just stay put?

six states, ten houses
how do i wake up without the bugle call?
why do people stare at me when i stand
with my hand over my heart for an anthem that's
only playing in my head,
how do i fall asleep without taps singing me a lullaby?

six states, ten houses
how can i even call myself a dandelion
when dandelions have roots?

# Overwatch

The road between the two bases was so heavily IED'd it had become known as Route Irish because you were lucky to survive a trip back and forth. Traveling east at that hour, the glare from the sunrise made the man on the bridge appear almost angelic. Seconds later, I realized he was.

# Not Quite Salvation

William Tucker staggered out of the main house, into the din of the harvest festival that the master of the estate gave each year for all the residents of Sleepy Hollow. A band played in the gazebo as a breeze made its way up from the Hudson River, keeping everyone comfortable on this warm Indian summer afternoon.

William looked back and saw Judge Dobbs, his employer, straightening his jacket and taking deep breaths. A few minutes before, in the servant's quarters, the Judge was losing his temper with William for impregnating Daisy, the downstairs maid. Daisy had disappeared earlier that morning and the Judge raged at William's immoral conduct. He vowed to go to the courthouse in Tarrytown and sign a warrant to have William arrested for duping the impressionable young girl.

While Judge Dobbs was threatening William with prison, Horace Musselman was loading the cannon in front of the house. It would be fired to mark the end of the fall festival. He carefully measured out the powder and rammed it into place with the same efficiency as when he was a gunner in the New York 5th Light Artillery during the Civil War under Judge Dobbs' command. He longed to load one of the cannonballs he had stashed in the barn and see if he could still hit a target with the same accuracy he had back during the war, but the judge never let him have any fun.

William stumbled down the steps into the crowded festival. He did not hear the band, the people engaged in conversation, or the children running from game to game. Some man with more strength and virtue than him, had just rung the bell in a display of the real strength that William knew he lacked. The man that rang the bell was apparently not someone who would seduce a girl of sixteen, with promises of marriage and a life he never intended to give her, even after she submitted to his will. William realized that the Judge was right, that he was a man of low moral fiber.

He looked across the crowded lawn, past the tables of watermelon and drinks, past the booths of games, to the railroad tracks leading to the city and to the river just beyond. His legs wobbled as he descended the steep hill.

His mind was made up. Either a train would smash and end his unworthy life, or he would just walk into the water and end it. He would let the river take his body past the city and out into the Atlantic, never to be found, since he did not deserve a proper burial or any sort of remembrance after what he had done.

All the noises of the day combined into an echoed vibration inside his head. Everything to his periphery was hazy, as if the world had slowed its motion and had lost all adherence to the laws of time. He heard celestial music over the ringing in his ears. Was he already dead? The music grew louder as his foot toed the steel tracks. He stepped onto the gravel between the ties and waited for the singing angels to be replaced by the whistle of the train bound for Grand Central Station or Albany.

He closed his eyes and waited. He tried to remember the hymn from when his parents would walk him to the old stone church on Broadway when he was a boy. He hummed along as his memory found the second verse.

The angels began the chorus, "Shall we gather at the river . . ."

William looked north to Albany and south to the city. There was no sign of smoke on the horizon and no rattle of an oncoming locomotive. He was drawn again to the Hudson and began walking to the banks. He closed his eyes again as his first shoe filled with water. He was up to his waist, waiting for the depths to swallow him, stopping as small waves lapped against his chest. He tried to summon the will to go on, taking another deep breath and lifting his leg to finish what he had started.

He felt a hand on his forehead and another on the small of his back. A large man appeared in the corner of his eye; he was suddenly plunged under the water with the man holding him beneath the surface. He kicked and thrashed swam his arms in an attempt to get out of the water, but he had no balance and the man was very strong. Just as he was about to run out of air, he was lifted back to his feet. Gasping for air, he saw his attacker, the Reverend Fletcher from the First Baptist Church and behind him on the dock, his choir singing the praises of the newly baptized.

"You are saved!" the reverend declared as William blinked in disbelief.

Just as his head cleared and he was finally grasping what had happened, screams rained down the hill from the festival. He saw the crowd rushing for the front of the Judge's house. The screams continued.

The reverend began to run from the water and as he crossed the tracks, William felt compelled to follow. He barely had the strength to climb the hill. After forcing himself through the crowd, he saw Judge Dobbs on the ground with Dr. Jennings holding a blood-soaked towel to his employer's head. The Judge was not moving and looked to be barely breathing.

William grabbed the man next to him by the lapels.

"What happened?" he asked.

"David Templeton was showing off for a group of girls by ringing the bell at the test of strength. On his third try, he swung so hard the head of the sledge flew off and hit Judge Dobbs square in the head. He went down like a sack of potatoes."

As William pushed closer, Dr. Jennings stood, removed his jacket and covered the Judge's head.

"Our gracious benefactor is gone," the doctor announced to the stunned crowd.

Master Washington Irving Sneed, great-great grandnephew of the man who had made the town famous, aged seven years, was playing with his tin soldiers near the ceremonial cannon. Unfazed by the commotion by the house as he marched his favorite figurine to the end of the breach, where he pretended to shoot his toy's musket into the cannon, moving closer with each shot, until it teetered on the opening. Wash, as he was called, then promptly dropped the painted Revolutionary War soldier into the breach when his mother yelled at him to get away from there before he got his head blown off.

William headed to the barn to try to clear his mind. He should be dead, but instead it was Judge Dobbs who was growing cold. He decided to saddle a horse and get out of Sleepy Hollow before anyone could figure out that it was his debauchery that had caused the unfortunate chain of events. He mounted Midnight, Judge Dobbs' huge black stallion, and tried to ride off. He turned and looked back at the house and stopped because he thought he heard singing again.

That was because at the very same time, a grief-stricken Horace Musselman felt it was his duty to honor his fallen former commander. He walked over to the ceremonial cannon and started to sing the Battle Hymn of the Republic. By the time he got he got to "trampled out the vintage," the entire crowd was singing along with him.

When they the finished the verse, Horace lit the fuse on the cannon, which fizzed and stopped for a few seconds until it finally exploded, sending the tin soldier hurtling in the direction of the barn where the toy made contact with William's neck, taking his head off cleanly, sending it bounding down the hill, where it bounced through the window of the 6:15 express train to Albany and into the lap of Miss Daisy Downing.

She rang the bell for the conductor.

"Providence has delivered this piece of refuse; can you please see that it is properly disposed of?"

Spooked by the sound of the cannon, Midnight took off with his headless rider, across the lawn, the crowd politely clapping, as many commented about how realistic the tribute to the history of Sleepy Hollow was and that the reenactment seemed appropriate as the town was beginning to mourn the loss of their patron.

William's head spent an hour in the lost and found at the Ossining Station before the authorities finally arrived to begin their search for the rest of William. Midnight, with the most recent headless horseman galloped south, reaching the Bronx, before stopping outside a saloon, where the stallion squeezed in between the other horses for a drink at the trough.

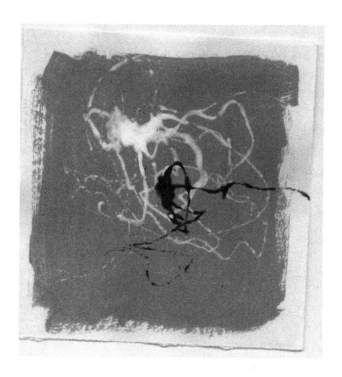

Pat Hambrick

# Standing Watch

All night
the dogs barked from the back pasture.
Again and again you went out
to look for whatever danger
lurked in the dark,
shotgun loaded and ready.
You found nothing
but signs that something waited,
hidden in the shadows:
the air was filled
with the wild, musky scent of a fox;
the geese had moved
to a pond closer to the house,
leaving a pile of downy feathers
on the bank of the far pond
as if one had barely escaped
from the intruder.

Sometime during the night
you realized, half asleep,
old habits were rising
like the pale moon outside our window:
roll-out-grab-the-gun-start-moving
had become one motion again –
a habit learned for survival years ago
when perimeter alert sounded.

At daybreak
wild creatures of the night
return to the burrows.
You come to bed
but I know you can't relax and sleep
after a night of standing guard
unless someone takes over the watch.
In the jungles of your dreams
we are never safe,
but the gun is not needed now.
You sleep soundly
as I take my turn at watch
in the faint glow of early dawn
armed only with a cup of coffee.

# Resonance

One steamy June afternoon several decades ago, I sat alone amid two hundred other soldiers in an outdoor stadium. Although we all wore identical uniforms, I didn't belong. I felt small and weak compared to the tough looking guys around me. As one of the few women in the group, I didn't fit the macho Army soldier mold. Doubts about my capabilities filled me as I listened to a first aid class. What had I gotten myself into?

In addition to first aid, the college juniors attending Reserve Officer Training Corps summer camp practiced everything Army—chemical warfare, marching and marksmanship, group physical fitness and precision bunk bed making. Each of us took a turn being in charge to prepare us for our future roles as Second Lieutenants responsible for forty other soldiers.

In an instant, Fort Bragg's sweltering sunshine transformed into a torrential downpour. I was already drenched by the time I threw on my Army-issued poncho.

Rain pelted me while Jim, the cadet in charge for the day, called our platoon into military formation. As part of our training, we always paraded from place to place. The person in charge had a chance to practice giving orders to move a large group. I trudged into place in the second row, ready to march back to the barracks a few miles away.

From his spot leading the platoon, Jim commanded, "Forward march," and we all stepped forward at the same instant.

We took a few steps in silence before Jim raised his voice. "Your left, your left, your left, right, left." He used a common military cadence call, also known as a "jody," to keep us in step.

I sighed. At this rate we'd be out here twenty more minutes. From my thighs down, I was already a squishy, sopping mess. My poncho's sticky nylon clung to my arms like a second skin and rain dripped from my cap brim, splashing my face. I wallowed in self-pity, focusing on a rivulet zig-zagging down the olive-colored poncho of the cadet in front of me.

My path to the Army had been similarly meandering. In my freshman year, my dad pointed out that ROTC classes substituted for some of the gym credits my liberal arts college required. I hated gym. In high school I had a reputation as a klutz which left me staring at my shoelaces while everyone else in class was picked for teams. Never chosen, I only ended up on a team by default.

Dad's proposition sounded ridiculous at first. As a "girly-girl," more interested in reading a mystery novel or sewing a pretty skirt than in sports, camping, or anything physical, I had no intention of joining the Army. But Dad tapped a finger on the fine print, which explained that I could avoid gym with no military obligation simply by taking two semesters of ROTC class. Sold.

What went wrong with my plan? Why was I out in the rain, cursing everyone and everything, including my beloved Dad? When I started junior year the US economy looked dismal. And I had trouble settling on a college major, let alone a post-graduation career path. Army leadership skills, Dad convinced me, would add to my future résumé. With some hesitation, I signed up. My three-year Army obligation would begin after graduation the following May. First, though, I had to survive summer boot camp.

As if answering my unspoken prayer, Jim ratcheted our speed. "Double time," he said. In response, I took another complete step. Left. Right.

On the next beat, Jim said, "March," and, as one, our unit sped up to a slow, steady jog. To match the pace, he switched to a faster, more singsong jody. "I want to be an Airborne Ranger." Jim's gruff voice was in sync with my miserable mood.

Our tone lackluster, the rest of us echoed back, "I want to live a life of danger." Nope, not me. I wanted a life of comfort and convenience, not misery. I should never have joined the Army.

"Sound off," Jim called.

"One, two," we answered.

The rhythmic squelching of many feet served as backdrop to my inner complaints. Why me? My fatigue pants rubbed against the poison ivy rash on my legs, making me grit my teeth against the itch.

I had no choice but to persevere. When I signed on the dotted line, I committed to three years, no matter what. I had to figure out how to make it through summer camp, plus three more years. I sighed again, daunted by the endless stretch before me.

The first jody ended. For several moments, the sound of drumming rain hitting ponchos melded with boots stomping in unison, creating a haunting, lonely rhythm.

In time with our running, Jim began to sing.

"Michael, row the boat ashore," his rich voice rang out.

I opened my eyes wide and lifted my head. No one ever sang a non-military song. I felt a tickle of anticipation trill down my spine in the second before we responded.

"Alleluia," I sang, adding my soft tone to the deep voices rising around me.

Music swelled. My spirits lifted.

We began singing in rounds, answering each other instead of responding to Jim. Verses and alleluias overlapped. Where before I'd slogged, now I glided. My heart soared along with our choral resonance.

Male voices flowed, deeper and more sonorous than before. The downpour accompanied our choir while our pounding feet kept time.

Despite the drenching rain, my gloom evaporated as if a switch had flipped. We became the music. All of us together shaped the song.

I no longer felt alone. Instead of being left until last, I belonged on the team, contributing to its spirit and vitality. Certainty enveloped me that I would survive the summer. In that moment, I felt capable and sure, almost as if I could fly, and I wanted to keep running forever.

Through sheets of rain, the barracks appeared, welcoming me home. Although our song and the run, came to an end, the magic of that day endured. After almost three decades in uniform, I often think back to that soggy run and hold onto the moment I blossomed from a teenaged girl into a soldier. Even now, years later, when the rain pours down, I can still hear singing and feel the soaring sound.

Holly Apperson

# Udu

He starts with gray clay.
His hands hear the udu's form—
a drum from earth, fire-born.

He kneads it,
feels what it needs to rise,
molds its timbre,
shapes the chambers where air will flow.

Hands gloved in slick clay,
he spins the pottery wheel,
smoothes the tooled grooves,
conducts the breath of future music.
After the kiln-fire,
below the udu's glaze,
earth rises, hushes across his fingers.

His spirit hums river over rock,
splashes in its vase-like basin.
Its voice deepens, swims up
from sculpted hollows,
slows on the trek, pulses
through the narrow neck
till finally, the low notes glug,
flow into us like water from a jug.

Tap its rhythm, rub its heartbeat—
scatter of foaming sea
sweep of light rain
in fingertip patter.

Palm-percussed, its bell-bottom
hints a xylophone ring.
Strike the rim—
a slight buzz, cymbal-ting.

Primal wind sloshes
in a genie bottle—
the udu's belly swells with song.

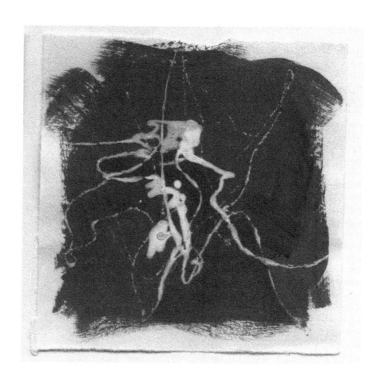

# Jane

"Lay me in the lilies when I die," you told them. "Lay me in a wooden box."

They drank the wine of your life in iron cups, deep, long dregs, and tasted it on their tongues. Bitter, sweet. All around them, the black crepe and the shed tears. The unnerved silence, the peering over the open coffin lid and asking: where are you?

Where are you, indeed? Or rather—where are you not? You walk between them but they can't see you brush their shoulders with yours and they don't feel you. You are above and below.

You are among them, and yet so very far away.

You'd heard about God. Of course you had. You'd been pressed between the pages of the Good Book in Bible Studies and looked Judas in the eye. You'd seen postulants become nuns and smiled when priests were dragged from their altars. You'd been fed His commandments, but they were too sour to swallow.

You'd heard about God. But this just wasn't it.

You're afloat in neither space nor heaven. But it's not nothing, either. It just . . . is. There's nothing above, nothing below. Only behind.

*You travel back.*

How did you come to be here? You glance back. You remember now. There was a loosening, a soft loosening, and a slow and fragile drifting up. There were stars, or something like stars, floating beside your eyes, and you tried to catch them and hold tight, but no—not yet. There was still so much looking back to do.

In some memories, you are alone. In hallways. Alleyways. All sorts of ways: lost, adrift, bruised. In others, there are arms to push, lift, hold you. In other moments, you are engulfed. By water (you'd always loved the Atlantic), by hands (you needed them to cradle you when your brother's casket—a sort of cradle—sank to the earth below), by fear (the greatest of all came when the light left you at last).

Your wedding day. Your kid's wedding day. The day you saw your brother for the last time. As a child, playing marbles in the gutter—glinting gems rolled in the mud. As a teen, sitting alone in a dim gymnasium all dressed up in streamers for prom. As an adult, lying awake at night, your eyes full of dark ceiling, wondering if you'd ever sleep. Wondering, wondering.

*You wonder.*

Three years old. Your first memory. The feverish eyes of a robed priest crucify you even in the farthest pew. When he raises his arms to speak, he's a cross silhouetted against the stained-glass window. "Life is a journey to heaven or hell. To walk the road of sin is to walk the road to the devil." Even then, you wondered what path he led, and where he was leading you.

Eight years old. Your lost cat—Dad said it was, anyhow—isn't lost at all, only ripe with worms. Your father takes his Winchester from its place above the mantle and shoots the tabby dead. *No more misery.* You find the cat's body, swarming with maggots and death, but you can't bury it; you only stare, for hours—or minutes—into that gaping bullet hole.

Ten years old. You're a passenger. You sit, eyes on the hearse ahead of you, as your father's station wagon drags itself along the line of black cars. Your brother was walking by your side three days ago. Now, you're following him.

Thirteen. Your mother, at night, at the kitchen table. She's crumpled like tissue paper as she holds your father's photograph. He's in uniform, smiling in black and white. He was quick to follow your brother. They've probably been through what you're going through right now.

Sixteen years old. Not your first kiss. It was memorable enough, it seems, for you to remember it.

Eighteen. Alone, shivering in an apartment you were once so proud to rent. The radiator's shot. Snow glazes the window. Your fingers are bruised a cold, icy blue. It's a long drive to your mother, the widow, who begged you to stay. You weren't ready, and she told you that. *She told you that.* "You've learned the hard way, haven't you?" she clucked, but she was smiling beneath her curlers as she let you inside the home you'd fled.

Twenty-something. Maybe twenty-two. Someone bumps into you—hard—on a busy summer street and doesn't say a word. You can't, not for the life or death of you, figure out why you'd remember that now.

*—(of all things)—*

Thirty. A delivery room: a sharp smell ringing in the air, of blood and sweat and screams. Your first child. Then a second; you weren't expecting twins. You smile all the same while you fight to scratch an itch at the back of your brain: you didn't plan on two college funds.

106

## ODET

Fifty-three. A mid-life crisis compels you to dye your hair an ungodly shade of green. Thinking it would only last the holiday, you didn't realize how long *permanent* really meant. Your boss gives you hell. You're tempted to give it right back. But you never were the sparring sort.

Sixty-four. On the porch, your hand wrapped around the one you've promised yourself to, your wedding bands aglow in the evening air. You haven't been so happy in so long. You wonder how long your smile will last.

Eighty. The lights of your room at the retirement center are too bright. As you ask the nurse to "hush them up, for Christ's sake," you glance out your window to the generous view of slogging city traffic. But outside, in a terracotta pot, the lilies are standing proudly today, their white petals smiling like freshly-polished teeth in the smog. You'd like to die with them. Bones creaking, you turn to the silver-haired nurse, who stands faceless in the doorway. You never could remember faces. But you remember her name. Jane. "Lay me in the lilies when I die. Lay me in a wooden box." It's the same thing you murmur one week later when your family—what's left of it, anyway—comes for the last time (just in the nick of it) to watch you let go.

They gave you your lilies.

They gave you your wooden box.

You didn't bother asking for anything else. Not even to be remembered.

*(why o why couldn't you have just asked for one more thing—?)*

You read something once, somewhere, that sometimes your brain makes up—or made up—memories. Fills in the gaps with fiction. Those blank margins with markings erased, or had never been scribbled in in the first place (but you wouldn't know that).

How truthful is the afterlife? Was it Dad who shot the cat, or your brother? Surely you couldn't forget a thing like that. Did you even go to prom? You never saved a corsage. Hadn't your kids been born at home? Were they truly lilies? Was your box of wood? Did they even bury you at all?

*—was her name Jane?*

# Jungle Prada

What happened to that boy-dust
    that stuck to your dirty feet
        when you threw baseballs and Frisbees just west of 66th Street,
        slinked through sandy trails of old Pinellas like an adolescent bobcat?

Even now, there is your sweat-sweet neck,
    eyes as clear as blue sandbar ripples,
        hands so delicately masculine.

In this, your sixth decade, you refuse to sketch or fish or strum,
    choosing instead, mostly solitude,
        the roux of sound on a page,
        the company of women you once loved.

Yes, we both know that there are oodles of bitter avengers who outshout
    the sounds of their sins
        with the taa-da-ta-taa of dirty tap dancing,
    and a new century's army of red elves with ray guns,
        miscible chemicals dropped more casually than sarin, VX, or mustard.

Nonetheless, you are as seeded and ancient as any pomegranate.
And here I am, not asking you to catch me fish to fry,
    but just to hum three bars of Oscar Peterson's "Laura,"
        or maybe that old folk tune about "coming 'round the mountain."

# Knight of Sorrows

Erik, your camera light scanned this century's Nordic land,
      capturing a snowy field of seventeen headless reindeer.
I am not sure if I can imagine the wet heat of their exhalations,
            and I wonder if Dunedin's curator could. Yet
            she and I may both believe
            that the racks of antlers absent from your photograph
                create an angle as acute
                as last year's memory of Sanibel's whale shark,
                this month's news of five-thousand starved puffins.

My sister insists that Hamlet would have cried again,
      there in Denmark.
      And that Ophelia's madness has come to us all.
She asks if we dare equate these losses with the decomposing boy soldiers
            in Congo,
                broom-swept Guatemala,
            the tiniest bodies of Yemeni hunger.

Exhausted as we are by first-world bullets, third-world despots,
                the fallout from those long-rotted explorers,
     we have nothing to do but return to our rebar and mortar,
            hunker down like roosting hens in a hurricane,
thankful for the songbirds and grasshoppers, the blue sky and baby bears
              taking first dibs on wild-caught salmon.

*Island Time*, W. Chris Dotson

# Bird Watching

Two parrots fucking on a wire
without a care to the traffic below,
their love on display for all to admire
or at least those waiting on *green* to go.

A bird of a different kind of feather
turns the AC a bit more cold.
He's down here to escape the weather
but he just can't escape being old.

A mother with a toddler in the seat behind
pulls a Goldfish from her hair,
dreams of the career she didn't find
and wonders how she got here from there.

A college student on her way
to the happiest place on earth,
has tuition and bills to pay
but minimum wage is all a princess is worth.

They watch the birds and dream of flight,
as thoughts escape the path they're on.
Await a change, here's the light.
Accelerate, now they're gone.

The people you leave keep on living
Their lives going on without you
That hole that you left they just fill in
While hardly thinking about you.

The text that you sent sits unanswered
For days or weeks at a time
You think that maybe the phone's disconnected
But you know in your heart that it's fine.

You remember the texts
Six messages deep
When the distance between you
Was just one or two streets.

But now your phone doesn't ring
Though these cans need no string
And only one call
Could make the distance.

Seem small
Point A to Point B, and that line in between
to reach your destination,
the measurements unseen.

Are we there yet, have I arrived
and achieved the achievable dream?
Can success be measured by an average or mean?

Three kids, a house, a dog and still
grasping for that something left to fulfill
this longing in my soul to be more until

your embrace.

Your hands the points, your arms the line
around me, encircled

*this* circle

is fine.

# Veiled Interpretations

*Don't throw away this note. You'll be sorry.*

Grace read the handwritten sentences twice. Then again. The penmanship was rough, jerky, the t's and l's like ominous spikes on an EKG. Or a polygraph.

The lined paper had fluttered from the pages of a paperback as she'd removed the book from the confines of the Little Free Library, a brightly painted wooden box on a pole that had been set up along the walking path to serve as a free book exchange. How many times had she passed the wooden box—and others like it—without peering inside? A dozen, at least. Nobody would give away perfectly good books for free, she thought, unless they weren't worth reading.

But this day Grace was feeling particularly bored. She and her husband Jay had recently relocated to the quiet coastal town, and it hadn't been her first choice. She'd been campaigning for Colorado, the land of crisp mountain vistas and low humidity. But Jay had little seniority at his company, and he had to take what was offered if he wanted to advance. And even Grace had to admit the winters were nice in the Southeast. She liked taking midday walks in January without worrying about the threat of frostbite.

Still, the absence of old friends and familiar places left her empty, and loneliness could cause one to act out of character. So on a whim, she'd popped open the door of the box, pulling from it the first book that caught her eye: Sigmund Freud's *The Interpretation of Dreams*. The puzzling note had fallen, quite literally, into her lap.

Now what? A joke? Was somebody watching?

Superstition wouldn't allow her to throw the note out, so she did the only thing she could think to do—tuck it back in the book and walk away. Quickly.

For several days Grace avoided taking the same route on her walk to work, not wanting to pass the Little Free Library again. She knew she'd be tempted to open the same book, if it was there, to see if the note was gone. But after a week she felt silly for letting her fears control her. She was not one to fall for tricks and hoaxes. So squaring her shoulders, she purposefully walked toward the little wooden box and checked its contents. The book was still there. Not a lot of interest in Freud, apparently. Quickly, before she could change her mind, Grace grabbed the book by its covers and held it upside down. A note floated to her feet and landed face up.

*I knew you'd come back. I've been waiting.*

Stunned, she stared down at the missive that was threatening to blow away in the soft breeze from the Gulf. She should let it go. But a vague tickle had emerged in the base of her abdomen, and with a jolt she recognized it as the thrill of excitement—like the panic of vertigo near the edge of a mountain cliff or the anticipation of a roller coaster's impending descent. She scooped up the paper and shoved it in her pocket.

The first note had made her feel uneasy. *You'll be sorry.* Sorry for what? Who was this guy—she felt sure the notes were written by a male, although she couldn't say why—and what did he think he would do to her if she threw away his note? But the second message had left her feeling more curious than fearful. *I knew you'd come back.* So he was watching her then.

She shivered slightly in spite of the sun. Should she call the police? Tell Jay?

A few blocks from home, she realized she'd do neither. She'd forget about it. Put it behind her. Take another route to and from work so she wouldn't be tempted to look for another note. She was foolish for having looked a second time. She had been bored and restless, that's all. The stress of relocating and renovating their new home was exhausting, and friendships were slow to make. An uninspiring office job filled her days. Dinners were afterthoughts—a sandwich while watching the news online or scouring the ads for furniture bargains while Jay worked late. So it wasn't at all odd that in her boredom she'd found the mysterious disruption a bit thrilling at first. But now she was done with it. Intrigue was not an expected part of her life, nor was it welcome. She'd simply put it out of her mind.

★ ★ ★

For the first time in weeks, Jay was in the kitchen whipping up some dinner when Grace got home from work.

"Surprise!" he said, bowing slightly in her direction. "The master chef is in residence."

"Great! What are we having?" She was more than a little hungry, but Jay was no more of a chef than she was.

"Grilled cheese and tomato soup." He dramatically flourished an empty tin soup can.

She smiled grimly. Not only did tomato soup give her heartburn, she knew she'd be stuck with the dirty dishes, few as they were. "How was work?"

"Not bad. Same old thing."

She waited for him to ask about her day, and when the query wasn't forthcoming, she changed her mind and decided to tell him about the note. Maybe it would make him a little jealous. "I found another one of those weird notes today. You know, like I told you about a few weeks ago. In the Little Free Library."

Jay was already hunched over his soup bowl, carefully sipping the steaming liquid from his spoon without a sound. She knew he wouldn't slurp if his life depended on it. She also knew she should appreciate the show of good manners but found it irksome.

"Do you want to know what it said?" she asked after a few minutes. "The note?"

"What does it matter? Just some weirdo with nothing else to do. I don't know why you looked in that box anyway. Who knows where those books even come from? They could be riddled with germs or stained with . . . well, I don't even know why you bothered. It's gross."

Grace bristled at his condemnation. "It's no different than a regular library, Jay. People take those books home, too, and cough and sneeze all over them before they bring them back."

"Well, not that I use real libraries, either—because I agree with you, by the way—but at least those books are checked out to people with actual names and addresses instead of anonymous creeps who leave threatening notes tucked between pages."

She had no retort for that. He was right, after all.

★ ★ ★

Grace's days passed slowly and without incident, stretching into weeks and then months. Most of the home repairs were finished, and the contractors had taken their payments and vanished. She still longed for the familiar landmarks of home, for old friends, for anything to break up the monotony of her life. Accustomed to the extreme seasonal changes of the Midwest, she didn't notice, at first, the mild differences that come with a change in subtropical seasons. She longed for a more dramatic transition, for the excitement that comes with an unexpected early spring snow or the first bright blossoms after the gray-brown of winter. But gradually she realized the bay breezes had grown warmer. She noticed more birdsong, followed by the loud nocturnal chorus of breeding frogs and the ever more obvious scurrying of tiny lizards. At last! Change was in the air, and she welcomed it.

She took a different route to work and back now, and she hadn't encountered a Little Free Library in some time. So the sight of a newly erected little library box—quaintly painted and decorated with glued-on baubles—abruptly stopped her in her tracks. Like the other one she'd encountered, it was set up on a pole in the grass near a sidewalk.

What could it hurt to take a look? She pulled open the little door and waited a moment for her eyes to adjust to its dark interior. At first the box appeared empty, but after a moment she could see a lone small paperback crouched in its farthest corner. She gasped.

Sigmund Freud's *The Interpretation of Dreams.*

As casually as she could, Grace glanced behind her and then to each side. A few patrons were waiting outdoors for a table at a nearby restaurant, but nobody was lurking. Nothing suspicious.

With shaking fingers, she carefully lifted the book. A slip of paper peeked from the top of the closed pages, perhaps to serve as a bookmark. Carefully, she opened the book to the indicated page. Someone had inked a blue line beneath the third chapter title: "A Dream Is the Fulfillment of a Wish."

Nothing really unusual there. A lot of people marked up their books. The bookmark was torn from a lined piece of paper, like the unsettling notes she'd found in the book before, but otherwise it was blank. Good. This was just a coincidence. Somebody had probably borrowed the book from the other little library and returned it here. No big deal. She flipped the bookmark over and looked at the back.

*I knew you'd look. Did you miss me?*

Grace flung the book into the box and slammed it shut. Slowly she stepped back, took a deep breath, and then took off as if the book could fling itself back out of the box and chase after her.

She was almost home when the thought occurred to her: two can play at this game.

* * *

The next morning, Grace took her old route to work and stopped at the Little Free Library where the first note had appeared. She looked in the box for the Freud book. Either her stalker hadn't had time to move the book back here yet, or he wasn't watching her closely and didn't know she had again changed her route. Fine. She'd purchased her own copy and brought it along just in case. Inside she'd tucked a handwritten note:

*Did you dream of me last night? I hope it was a nightmare, because I've called the cops.*

Of course she hadn't really called the police, because what could they do? But maybe the empty threat would scare the guy off.

The next day she walked the same route, and the next and the next. Each day, she stopped at the Little Free Library. Her book and note were still there. Other books had come and gone, having apparently caught the interest of passersby, but her Freud book remained. Good riddance to the creepy notes.

But by the end of the week, Grace was restless. She walked home along her secondary route and stopped at the little library where she'd last received a message. The first Freud book and its bookmark were gone.

Okay, she thought. The little game was over. She would go home to her husband, to her newly remodeled home near the Gulf, to her newly remodeled life in a new town. She would try harder to make new friends. Life was only boring because she let it be. She'd take up a hobby. Maybe join a book club or a writing group. Tutor kids, foster a pet. The options were endless.

Jay was lying on the couch, watching TV, when she got home. She snuggled in beside him, determined to add a little excitement to her life, starting with her marriage. "How was your day?" she asked.

"Better now," he said, leaning into the hug. "But I was just about to get a beer. Want anything? A glass of wine?"

"Sounds good." Grace stretched out on the couch as Jay went to get the drinks. Something small and boxy pushed into her back, and she reached between the couch cushions to pull out a worn paperback: *The Interpretation of Dreams.* Puzzled, she held out the book to Jay in silence when he reentered the room. He glanced at it briefly before handing her the wine but said nothing.

After all, what could he say? How to explain that the days and nights had become as stagnant for him as they had for her, that he sometimes yearned for his wild, impetuous pre-corporate days, when breathless young women and their doting mothers found him mildly menacing and alluringly dangerous?

They sat in the shadows without speaking as daylight faded, waiting for night and the next day and whatever would come after that. Finally, in the dark quiet that precedes the noise of a new beginning, Grace turned to look at his barely visible profile.

"Did you dream about me last night?" she whispered.

He was breathing deeply but his eyes were open, so she knew he wasn't asleep. Still he stayed silent. And then in the first light of dawn she saw it: a small wistful smile of hopeful longing.

"A dream is the fulfillment of a wish," he said softly.

# Disconnections

First of all, I should make the following clear: I hated my job, I despised the man I worked for, and I wasn't that crazy about the bank, either. Which makes the whole "saving the bank" thing a little strange.

First Penobscot County Bank is a typical small community bank. It has branches in Bucksport, Searsport, Vinalhaven, Brewer and Belfast. Our headquarters are on State Street here in Bangor, with assets of one-hundred and thirty-five million, and a past that goes back one-hundred and sixteen years.

My name is Jerome Gephardt, and I am twenty-nine years old, all of which has been spent in and around Bangor. I took a job with First Penobscot after working two years at a furniture rental place. Before that, I majored in social studies up at Orono. Not much in my past screams "hero."

After five years on the platform in the nearby Brewer branch, I was tired of dealing with customers like old Mrs. Lacroix who wanted me to check her monthly interest calculation, daily. Mr. Getchell would inquire about CD rates every few days, as if the timing of his twenty-five-thousand-dollar investment would alter his quality of life. All the regulars my parents' age would come in and ask me about my mom. "No, Mrs. Levereaux, Mom has not come home from the institute in Augusta. They don't think she's quite ready after this last incident."

I sat there behind that desk, vulnerable to whomever might venture through the double-doors, while I just wanted to be invisible. The guys I went to high school with would regularly come in and make fun of me wearing a tie while they made twice what I did skidding logs or putting in time on the lobster boats. So, was it any wonder that when Harold Haynes was promoted to Treasurer and the job in the Wire Room at the main office opened up, I applied? The retail head, Old Whitefish, begged me to stay in the branches. "You're a natural, Jerome," as if being nice to customers was so difficult. But I persevered, talked to the President, Jack Lyon, and even was nice to Harold, who was only three years older than me. Harold's age probably meant I would be promoted to Treasurer when I was sixty-two, but I desperately wanted out of the branches. I wanted to be a back-office nobody; just do my job and collect my semi-monthly paycheck.

After nearly a month of waiting on tenterhooks, I got the letter. Either they couldn't find anyone else, or I just wore them down. I let out a loud "Wahoo" in the branch, but fortunately, it was around two PM and the branch was deserted. Denise Bates, yes, one of those Bates, and on whom I had a major crush, smiled across the empty branch at me from her teller's window.

"Did you get it, Jerry?"

"Sure did. I'm going to miss you all." The only thing I was going to miss was looking across the branch at her cheerful face, shoulder length dirty-blonde hair and those oh-so-cute freckles around her nose, "but I got to move ahead. Got to have a career, you know."

I kind of regretted that last comment, in case Denise thought I was disrespecting her job choice.

Denise smiled sweetly. "You'll do well, Jerry. You may not be the most ambitious guy I ever met at First Penobscot," which would have to be Harold, "but you have a good head on your shoulders. Don't forget us branch peons on your way up."

So, it is off to the Wire Room for the future hero. The Wire Room at First Penobscot sends and receives a total of about twenty wires a day. A wire is money, money in its purest form as ones and zeros transmitted over an encrypted phone line to the Fed in Boston, and from Boston to central banks in glamorous capitals and obscure nations around the world. A few buttons, a code word from me, and money would magically depart First Penobscot and arrived in Ulan Bator or wherever. The most-glamorous place I ever sent a wire was to San Francisco, but I did get a wire once from Paris paying for a planeload of lobsters. How cool is that for a Bangor boy?

Plus, as Harold is forever reminding me, once a wire is sent, it can't be recalled. I suppose you could ask for the money back, but good luck with that.

Well, after a few months, the whole "back-office nobody" gig felt a lot less-cool as I sat in the eight-by-eight room in front of my computer monitor. Especially as my room had no windows and no outside doors, lit only by a large overhead florescent light that constantly hummed. To get to my office I had to go through Harold's office, but by an immediate and unstated understanding, it became clear that I only left the Wire Room and transited

Harold's office once a day, for lunch. Harold was far too important to have the Wire Room Clerk flitting across his office. Oh, no, that would not do.

Within the year, I was bored out of my tree. I fantasized about blowing up the bank and creating slow and lingering deaths for Harold. "Don't make any mistakes today, Jerome," he would say as I entered the Wire Room in the morning. "Did you shut off the terminal?" he would query as I exited for lunch. Harold had been the Wire Room Clerk for three years; he apparently felt his experience, and the fact that he was my boss, gave him carte blanche to recite the obvious to me day after day.

Until my "hero" day, I sat in the Wire Room without incident. I would take my coffee and the newspaper in first thing in the morning, close the door to Harold's office, and inhabit my own little world. I read the paper and did both the Sudoku and the crossword while I waited for wires to come in. Wires from First Penobscot generally went out in two batches, one at around ten, when I would receive instructions from Harold's other clerk, Mike something-or-other, and again at around two-thirty before the books closed for the business day. Mike would knock on the door; I made sure the newspaper was put away before I let him in.

One Saturday, I explained my new job to Denise over breakfast at the Miss Waldo Diner. "Wires coming in have a tracking number, the name of who gets the money, an amount, and sometimes an account number. I tear the wire off the printer, fill out a deposit slip, staple them, and send both to Deposit Operations. Sometimes, I need to do a little sleuthing to figure out whose money it was, but it never takes more than a couple of minutes." First Penobscot isn't that big, and we don't have many customers who get wires. Mostly, they are the timber companies and the lobstermen's cooperative.

I continued, grinning as I explained that sending the wires was much more fun. "Once I receive instructions from Deposit Operations, I write up a credit slip. I make sure that customer had signed the wire instructions, with the bank name and the name and account number of the party to receive the money. I then look up the transit number and sign on my terminal. I enter my sign-on, password, a second password for extra security, you know, like you do on the teller system, then add in the wire details.

"Lastly, the wire isn't going anywhere without my secret eight-digit code. The security guy, Phil Olsen, gives me a new number on the first day of each month. After I enter the secret code, the printer prints off a confirmation, which I attach to the credit slip and send back to Deposit Operations."

Within a few months, I could do this whole job in my sleep. Which I am sure is what they were counting on.

As far as the "they," well, we don't rightly know who the "they" were involved in making me a hero. I'd send them a "Thank you" card if I did. The FBI thinks it was the Russian Mob. Denise and I joked that Harold was being blackmailed or was to get a share. Either way, "they" almost pulled it off.

The caper started when they painted Harold's office. The bank has a contract with Keener's Painting to paint the branches on Sundays, when they are closed, but they usually do the offices every five years or so during the week. No one noticed that Harold's office was scheduled to be painted at the same time as they were doing the main branch downstairs.

Old Mac, the Sunday guard, naturally let the guys dressed in Keener's overalls into Harold's office to paint. Harold and I returned on Monday to find a nice new coat of eggshell white on the walls and doors, including the door to the Wire Room. Joey Keener insists to this day that no one on his crew painted Harold's office, which we tend to accept on account of it was a much-tidier job than the branch received downstairs. And Old Mac couldn't pick Marlon Brando out of a line-up, let alone the guys he let into Harold's office.

Whatever happened in Harold's office, no one thought to give the unpainted Wire Room the once over. Everyone figures the door must have remained locked and Old Mac didn't have a key. But there it sat, attached under my desk, ticking away like a bomb in a James Bond movie. Just waiting for the right party to set it off.

Since the FBI got involved, they have showed the gizmo to me. It looks like a plain black computer modem, measuring perhaps two inches thick and four inches by six inches around, with the same four flashing lights as the one that sits on my desk. It had a small antenna that lay flat against the underside of my desk. I never saw one like it before, and you can be darn sure that I check under my desk every day since the big event. There hasn't been the appearance of a second flashing box so far.

My "hero" day was Tuesday, March 14th. It began routinely; I entered my room on time at nine accompanied by Harold's daily instructions with regards to mistakes, the not making thereof. I put my coffee on the desk, signed on to the terminal, put my feet up and began to read the *Bangor Daily News*.

I was busy reading a story about Augusta politicos when I happened to glance at the monitor. The cursor, with no prompting from me, was rapidly moving across the screen, typing out bank destinations for wires.

The first line was familiar; it was my normal destination prompt:

"100-424-100 Federal Reserve of Boston"

Then the amount began to fill in: five, fifty, five-hundred, five-thousand, fifty-thousand, five-hundred thousand, five million. It stopped at fifty million. The biggest wire I had ever sent was two-hundred thousand dollars.

The cursor sped on, unaided.

"For further credit to: Cayman Trust, Georgetown, Cayman Islands. Account number: 2236-1089547"

After a brief pause, the cursor again began to move.

"For further credit to: Hitchen Trust Co., Isle of Man. Account number: 212-2687-03004."

I sat mesmerized. I didn't even know you could send it beyond the first bank!

The cursor kept on typing "For further credit to:" sending the money on from the Isle of Man to Monte Carlo, then finally to rest in Zurich.

The magic cursor sped on, typing in the first digits of this month's secret security code.

Denise says it was the bravest thing she ever heard of, but she has to say that as we are getting married in the chapel at Bates College next June. "After all, Jerry, you had no idea what would happen when you went into action. You were decisive."

When I saw that cursor start typing my very-own secret code, which would send the bank's money wheeling from Bangor to Boston to Georgetown in the Cayman Islands to the Isle of Man to Monte Carlo to Zurich, I reacted like any boy who had spent his whole life in Bangor.

I pushed back my chair, stood up, dived under the desk, and yanked the computer power cord out of the wall. When I scrambled out from under the desk, I watched the monitor squeeze down to a pinpoint of light, then go dark.

The FBI said that the fifty million failed to depart First Penobscot at that very instant. Mr. Lyon, the President, also said that if the wire had gone out, it would have been the end of First Penobscot.

I was a hero, with my picture in the paper, a five hundred-dollar check from Mr. Lyon, a five thousand-dollar check from the FBI, and a ten thousand-dollar check from the American Bankers Association. I also collected a half-hearted "Way to go, Jerome" from Harold. Best of all, I got Denise.

I am still working in the Wire Room, though I am looking for something else. Special Agent Williams from Boston says he can put in a good word with FinCEN for me when there's a vacancy.

Back in the Wire Room, I have rigged up a piece of string tied to the power cord, with the other end taped to the surface of my desk. One yank from me, and that baby's shutting down again. I might try it tomorrow, if it's a slow day.

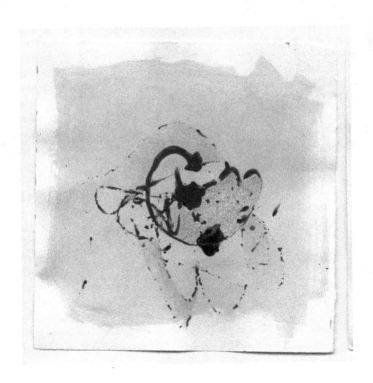

*Rotten Wonderland*, Alaina Virgilio

# Thither the Phoenixes Do Not Come Flying

I graduated from Pratt Institute in Brooklyn, New York during the mid-term in 1973 with a Bachelor's degree in Fine Arts. Because I achieved my credits and completed my classes during the dead of winter I left school and began working full time—as a waiter in an Italian restaurant called Joe's Place. I enjoyed the work, learned to cook and made what for those days was really good money. Most mornings I slept in and most afternoons I would read and get a little buzz on before work. What I wasn't doing—what I had stopped doing after three years of doing practically nothing else—was paint. As soon as school officially was over my mind officially shut down. Being a waiter or a cook was for me a no-brainer. Painting took thought, concentration and discipline. All that went out of me like air out of a balloon. Also, my girlfriend had broken up with me and so I had a lot of time to myself. The only obligation I had aside from showing up to work was walking my dog. Life had become very simple.

But life had also become numbing. I had zero inspiration and zero ambition and so I had no motivation aside from dragging my ass out of bed to feed myself and the pooch. I was avoiding some big choices and, unsure of what I wanted, I put off having to make any decisions until I absolutely had to. The choice of whether or not to go to grad school or start taking my paintings to galleries in the city or get a "real" job in the Manhattan art world were weighing heavily on my mind. There was, however, one thing gnawing at the back of my mind, drawing me away from these decisions: a strong desire to travel.

Up to that time I had spent almost my entire life in and around New York with a few trips to Canada and a lot of time in Miami, where my mother lived. I was a voracious reader and had taken to books where plots centered on travel and enlightenment. *The Razor's Edge, In Patagonia, On the Road, Siddhartha*, the novels of Lefcadio Hearn: these and many other novels about the journey struck a romantic chord in me that stuck in my brain like an itch I couldn't scratch. It seemed that grad school was not right and work was even less right for me. I knew I had to go someplace and I had the feeling that the visceral and tactile experience of the road would open me up to new worlds and experiences . . . and I'd find my muse.

In addition, I had also begun to learn about Zen Buddhism. I had awakened one morning to a lecture by Alan Watts on the radio and it piqued my interest. I read all of his books including *Zen Mind, Beginners Mind* and D.T. Suzuki's *Introduction to Zen Buddhism*. I read many other books from enlightened teachers. A journey to the Far East seemed imminent. And then I ran across a special novel, *Zen and the Art of Motorcycle Maintenance*, and the calling to the road was complete.

I bought a backpack, sold what I could, gave away the rest, packed the dog in the car and drove to Colorado. My sister was living in Boulder and with her help I was able to secure myself a cabin high up in the mountains for practically no cost. It was an old A-frame with a wood burning stove, no heat and my water source was a cold, clear creek running out behind the clearing. For one month I was a hermit and the only other being to talk to was my five year-old Irish Setter—and an occasional caribou. By day I'd chop wood, fetch water, draw and do small wood block carvings. In the afternoons I'd lay in a hammock reading. I'd take long walks in the valley near Caribou Ranch or up into the mountains where I could see the Continental Divide.

One hot August afternoon while reading in my hammock I heard the dog barking its head off and assumed he was chasing rabbits up near the ridge. Suddenly he ran past me in a panic. I thought he was being chased by a caribou or some larger animal but he just ran in circles barking like crazy. Within moments the sky turned greenish-black and then, just as suddenly, hail the size of golf balls began to rain down on us. We ran as fast as we could to the cabin and got under the eave just as the frozen pellets were turning into tennis balls.

We were having a grand adventure to be sure but after five weeks of solitude I realized I had to move on. I made my decision. Leaving both the car and dog with my sister and, using my thumb, hit the open road. For the next six months I hitchhiked my way around America. From Colorado I went north to Wyoming. There I met up with a group of young Vietnam veterans who with their girlfriends had tricked out a yellow school bus and were heading to Vancouver to start a commune. They invited me to join them and I eagerly joined their hippie caravan. By the time we arrived in California I knew that the commune life was not for me so I left those good people and hitched rides south to L.A. For a couple of months I traveled up and down the Pacific coast freely, sampled the local herbs, read my novels, wrote in my diary and drew in my sketchbook.

ODET

I settled in San Francisco, crashing with a friend of a friend in a third
floor apartment on Nob Hill. I even tried to get a job. At one point I was hired
to create a sexed-up comic book version of the Patty Hearst kidnapping. It
was gross and I had to quit. I fell in with a guy who had an air-conditioning
repair business but whose wife and sister-in-law wrote, produced and directed
porno films. They weren't very good but they made a lot of money.

The apartment I shared was leased to a guy who by day was a disciple
of Krishna Consciousness and by night a gay man who stalked the streets and
clubs of the City by the Bay looking for love. We had many, many lengthy
conversations about the meaning of life, religion and the illusiveness of true
love. In the fall his roommate returned and I had to find new quarters. I
decided to head to the Grand Tetons, where another old friend had settled
down. Once again I stuffed my backpack and stuck out my thumb.

Now about that backpack . . . It was a large blue JanSport that
comfortably held a sleeping bag, water bottle and had a secret lower pocket
where I kept my art supplies. Before leaving Brooklyn an old girlfriend had
given me a colorful appliqué patch with a lizard design from Honduras and I
had sewed it in the top of my pack for luck. Red, blue and orange, it popped
off the deep cerulean blue color of the canvas pack. I was very attached to that
pack.

I left San Francisco catching a few rides on Interstate 80 toward
Sacramento. By nightfall I hadn't gotten as far as the state capital and it was
getting dark and dangerous. I walked to the nearest exit and looked around
for a place to go but I was seemingly in the middle of nowhere. Near the road
there was a drainage ditch and a wire fence and I thought if I could get down
there and get comfortable I would catch some sleep until the sun came up
and head back to the highway. I put on my woolen coat, leaned against the
fence, and shut my eyes.

I awoke with a jolt as I felt something wet and fuzzy on my face. There
on the other side of the fence was a large Guernsey cow that had stuck its
snout through the fence and was licking my ear! I crawled out of the ditch and
found a Jack-in-the-Box about a mile down the road. I desperately needed to
wash my face and hands, go to the bathroom and get something to eat so I
carefully hid my pack in the ditch, lit a morning cigarette and walked down
the road.

About a half hour later I returned and shuffled back down into the
ditch. As I reached for my pack I stopped in awe. A large, absolutely gorgeous
dragonfly had landed on my pack and was sunbathing right on top of my

colorful patch. I felt compelled to allow him to stay there a while.

In Japanese culture the dragonfly is a very special insect and a symbol of good luck. In many cultures the dragonfly is a symbol of change and of enlightenment. It is also said the dragonfly can discern the nature of a man's soul. Finding this magnificent iridescent creature on my pack was indeed a good omen!

I sat in silence, looking at the creature and thinking about my own life. What did I want? Where would I go? Who would I be? Would this restlessness inside of me finally settle down? Where did I belong? How long would I stay on the road and where would this road take me?

After a while it began to get very hot and it was time to go. Mr. Dragonfly would have to get on his way too. I lit a cigarette and took off my coat. I went to shoo it away so I could open my pack and realized it was dead! It came to this spot as its final resting place. I was kind of stunned. Carefully I moved its body to the side and opened my pack. From the bottom I pulled out a box of wood engraving tools, emptied them into my coat and stuffed it all in the pack. I then ever so carefully put the dragonfly in the tool box and placed it in the secret compartment. Once everything was secure I walked back to the Interstate and stuck out my thumb.

Two days later I was sitting comfortably in a lodge in Teton Village having a beer with my friend. Two months after that I was renting an apartment on the Lower East Side of Manhattan. New York was my home and would be for most of the rest of my life. My path was set.

In only a few months' time I established myself as a successful illustrator of books, magazines and posters. At the top of my drafting table I kept the box with the now brittle dragonfly, a little worse for wear but still in one piece. One day I bought a lovely piece of Swiss Pear wood, sketched out the dragonfly and began to carve. A few days later I was making a limited edition of dragonfly prints. I took a line from Confucius for a title: "Thither the phoenixes do not come flying."

Over the years I have sold a few of those prints but mostly I have given them to family members or special friends. People have asked if I will make another print or another edition. I won't. It was a unique and critical moment in my life that I was able to capture and memorialize for myself. People may appreciate my design but I'm the only one who can have the visceral experience of what that little fellow meant to me. I have only one print left along with the wood block I printed it from. The dragonfly, nevertheless, lives inside my memory forever.

W. S. Ahlen

# Viburnum Lantana
## *The Wayfaring Tree*

From the beginning
Darkness streams to light
To breath, passions, carnal dreams,
Leading all to final loss.

A carefully wrought Eglantine life
Scorns transcendental thoughts
But growth begets change,
Rearranges the arc of being.

The human tide flows ceaselessly
From the valley's rift
Down mountains, past deserts
Unwavering to seas.

Thus does the wanderer go
Leaving behind inception with each step;
There are beginnings
But there is no journey's end.

Conception of body and soul,
The one eventually to dust
While uncaged, the spirit soars
Boundless, unfettered.

Thought and being, the veil is lifted,
The nameless wayfarer's illumination,
Voyaging to the placeless paradise
Where beginnings have no end.

# Point A to Point C

The auditorium was stuffy. Strangers surrounded me. I felt like a fraud. The words *I don't belong here* floated through my brain. I was convinced the hurricane warnings that had caused the cancellation of yesterday's classes had been a personal omen. Replaying my father's supercilious comments from childhood made me feel even worse. "Don't waste your time on college," he had scoffed repeatedly. "You'll end up a housewife, and you don't need a fancy degree for that." In rare letters after he and Mother divorced, he never failed to remind me that no one in our family had gone to college.

Although I was a member of two honor societies and had earned a college prep diploma, I was academically unprepared for a university curriculum. I had not taken Algebra II, trigonometry, chemistry, or physics like students who assumed college to be their natural destination. Instead, I had opted for courses in typing, shorthand, Business Math, and Business Machines in order to prepare for a secretarial position.

My steady boyfriend and I had devised a plan. He would earn his degree while I lived at home, worked, and saved money not only for our wedding but also for a down-payment on a house. All that changed, however, when I noticed him flirting with several of my college-bound girlfriends, while I faded into the background. It suddenly dawned on me that he and I would have little in common if I skipped college. In fact, I was sure he would probably fall for a co-ed and lose interest in me altogether.

On the weekend after this epiphany, Mother and I filled out a college application and loan papers in triplicate. As a result, seven months later, here I sat in a crowded auditorium watching a nervous, young professor blow into a staticky microphone. Although he spoke with little expression, I took copious notes in shorthand and planned my academic strategy. I recalled a stern warning Mrs. Blalock, my senior English teacher, had given our class more than once. "An A in high school equals a C in college." Certain that As at USF were out of my reach, I determined to earn a C average during my first trimester.

During the first meeting in each subject, I jotted down detailed requirements for projects and papers, along with their due dates. I lugged my books to the dining hall each day and ate dinner with my boyfriend, which was practically the only time we spent together. After the meal, I headed to the library, and he returned to his room at Beta Hall. I always occupied a corner table on the library's fourth floor to avoid distractions and remained until a few minutes before closing time. Once in the dorm, I resumed studying, while my roommate faced a wall and snored peacefully.

As a part-time student assistant in the university's Procurement Office, I worked twenty hours a week between classes and learned to manage my time carefully. Although I relished all aspects of college life, my boyfriend spent most of his time playing cards. He soon confided to me his intention to quit school and enlist in the Navy to avoid the draft. I, on the other hand, enjoyed most of my classes and had adapted well to a hectic schedule, new friends, and sudden independence. I also pleased Mother by inviting my seventh-grade sister to spend a few weekends with me on campus. By mid-term, I was considering taking fifteen hours during the summer and working full-time on breaks between trimesters.

While home for Christmas Break, I checked the mailbox every afternoon. One day the long envelope I'd been waiting for appeared on top of several others. It was from USF and was addressed to Mother. I ripped it open and yanked out the flimsy rectangle, then raced into the kitchen and jumped frantically up and down as I waved the paper in front of Mother. She stood up, laid the potato peeler down, and stared at the paper in my hands. Creases appeared on her forehead. She gave me a puzzled look as she gazed at the worst report card I had ever received. I, however, was sporting a grin so wide my cheeks ached. I could hardly believe my good fortune! I had earned a C in Freshman English, The American Idea, and Biology 101. In addition, the A in Introduction to Sociology had raised the D in Probability Theory. In short, I had earned exactly a 2.0—a C average! I had moved from point A to point C.

Unlike my past, the journey into the future teemed with endless possibilities. The most amazing part was the realization that I had already taken the first step.

# From the Dugout

I wanted to stand well,
knees flexed, arms loose,
anticipate his pitch,

hold the bat ready,
know the sweet spot
(no junk, no sting).

In dreams, in practice,
our game was play;
we danced around the bases.

I was not ready for the curve
he threw, body blow:
"You are not a player."

Hard hit, hurting,
I dropped the bat,
the ball, the game.

# Old Kidnappers Trail

"We didn't think we'd be needing tools when we decided to bike a few miles down Old Kidnappers Trail," I said. "So, we didn't bring any. Big mistake." I look around the table at the expectant faces of my brother and parents as they wait for my story.

I sigh. I don't want to relive the terrible events of last night, but my parents want to know and, since my sister Elisabeth is still sleeping, it's up to me.

My mother had said to be back before dark. My dad had suggested that we take tools in case of a breakdown. And we all had agreed that my older brother Tyler would open the door when we got home. Then, with Jennica's mom in the back seat, my parents had driven off to an important conference.

So I had biked off with my sister and my friend, knowing it wouldn't matter if we came home a little late because our parents wouldn't be home and there was no way Tyler wouldn't pay any attention, either.

"Hey, Macy," says Tyler. "Are you going to keep staring into space or are you going tell us what happened?"

I take a deep breath and begin my story.

★ ★ ★

We had just finished biking five miles down Old Kidnappers Trail and were heading back. Elisabeth and my friend Jennica rode side-by-side in front of me. Elizabeth's blond hair streamed behind her, the pink-and-white pom-poms on her pink bike sparkled in the mid-April sun. Jennica's long black ponytail matched the tires on her dark blue bike. They talked as they rode along.

Oblivious to the conversation in front of me, I was admiring the leafy trees, blue sky, and the long shadows cast by the setting sun. Just enough time to get home before dark.

"Hey, guys! Look, no hands!" Elisabeth shouted. Then she swerved out of control and toppled into the grass. Before I could ask if she was OK she jumped to her feet.

"Why did you guys stop?" She hopped on her bike, only to get off again and try to push it. Worry filled her light brown eyes. "The back wheel won't move!"

I got off my bike and examined her back wheel. The brake was jammed. It would take forever to get home with a broken bike. Jennica suggested fixing it. It seemed simple enough, but we didn't have any tools. We were in an adventurous mood, so we didn't mind. We laughed when Jennica called it "our first bike accident."

When the excitement calmed, I looked up at the glorious colors of sunset. We wouldn't get home before dark now.

I remembered my parents' warnings about being out after dark on Old Kidnappers Trail. These tales were mostly for Elisabeth because she was young and reckless. I never paid much attention to the stories of the bad people who supposedly come out at night and kidnap girls! After all, even though it may have happened before that didn't mean it would happen to us.

I shuddered and glanced at Elisabeth's bike.

"Jennica," I said, "Call Tyler. Tell him to bring the tools."

Jennica instinctively reached into her pocket to pull out her phone. Her face went pale. "I don't have it."

Elisabeth bounced on her bike seat. "Why are you two so scared? Come on! This is an adventure."

An adventure. I hadn't thought of it that way. We could be adventurers like the people in the books. And why couldn't we get home in the dark? People in books did stuff like that.

"We could send someone ahead," I suggested.

Jennica shook her head in the gathering darkness. "It's best if we stick together."

I didn't argue. Sticking together was a better plan.

"We could leave the bike here," Jennica suggested.

"No way!" Elisabeth shouted, putting her fists on her hips. "That's my bike and my dad just got it for me."

So we went on, each pushing a bike, taking turns with the broken one.

We tried to hurry, but it was useless. We had to half-carry it. We were soon sweating.

Dusk came and then total darkness. Clouds covered the moon. In the gloom, everything looked different. The trail loomed dark and foreboding. The wind whispered an eerie song. The trees morphed into monsters that shifted in the cool night breeze.

After walking to exhaustion, we sank down into the cool grass.

"We must be nearly there now," Elisabeth said with tired optimism.

"No," I replied. "We're not nearly there and we won't be for a long time."

"Maybe Tyler will come and get us. He had to notice we didn't return."

I hoped Elisabeth was right, but Tyler sometimes lost track of time when playing video games.

We lay in the grass, resting. I drifted in and out of a light sleep. I woke up shivering. Elisabeth and Jennica were sleeping beside me. We had been laying there for who knows how long.

I looked down the trail, hoping to see Tyler. My heart sank. Why hadn't he come to get us? I wondered. The realization hit me like a blow to the gut. Tyler wasn't coming.

★ ★ ★

"Now wait a minute" Tyler cries, "Of course I—"

My dad gives Tyler a stern look. "You can explain later, son. Please continue, Macy."

I nod and continue.

★ ★ ★

"Jennica, get up," I said. "We have to go."

Jennica opened her eyes. "He's not coming, is he?"

I shook my head, then woke Elisabeth. She moaned, "Why did you wake me up? It's not morning yet."

"The sooner we get home, the sooner you can go to bed," I told her.

"But I want to go to bed now."

It was clear to me that she didn't want to get up and it would take a lot to persuade her. Then I had an idea.

"Elisabeth," I coaxed. "Remember, this is an adventure. Do adventurers ever give up and just go to sleep?"

Elisabeth perked up. "No." She hopped to her feet and we were on our way.

After a time, I stumbled in the dark and nearly fell into a ditch. "Whoa," I said, trying to steady myself. Then I remembered that there were steep ditches on either side of the trail within two miles of home. Two miles! The thought gave me courage as I made my way back to the asphalt path. "Don't worry, guys. We're almost there."

Neither Jennica nor Elisabeth responded. Elisabeth struggled with her broken bike. I traded with her.

As we progressed, the distance between Jennica and my sister and I increased.

A rock clattered down into the deep ditch behind me. I looked ahead for Jennica, who was nowhere to be seen. I stopped pushing and turned around. My heart beat so hard, I was sure whoever was behind me could hear it. Out of the blackness a shadowy figure appeared, walking slow and deliberate. I squinted, unable to tell who it was in the darkness.

The person stumbled and fell into the ditch, letting out a scream that was cut short by a dull thud. I gasped. The scream sounded like a girl.

I dropped my bike and ran over to ditch. I peered down.

"Jennica, is that you?" I called.

No reply. The crescent moon peeked out from behind the clouds. Something dark blue lay in the ditch. It was Jennica's bike.

I scrambled down and knelt beside Jennica. She lay unconscious, with her head resting on a rock.

"Elisabeth! Get down here now. I think Jennica might have gotten a concussion."

My bike appeared above the ditch and toppled in, narrowly missing me and Jennica. Elisabeth landed right behind it.

"Elisabeth," I growled.

"Sorry."

I shook my head. I didn't have time to be angry. "Do you remember the time that you were running at the pool and what Mom told you about concussions?"

"Yeah, they make you forget stuff and they can kill you if they're bad enough."

"Oh, no. We need help."

Then an idea hit me. It was a terrible idea but I had no choice.

"We can't wait for someone to rescue us, and we can't leave her here," I said. "So, I'm going to get help. Elisabeth, you stay with Jennica."

"You can't go alone," cried Elisabeth. "What if you get kidnapped?"

"I won't," I said, trying to sound confident.

"There must be another way."

"If you know one, I'd be happy to hear it."

Elisabeth looked stumped. "Well at least take your bike."

I studied the sides of the ditch. They were too steep, "I can't push the bike out. I'll have to go on foot."

I looked at Elisabeth. She would be relatively safe here. Steep sides of the ditch would hide her from the sight of any passing kidnappers and the clouds would provide extra cover. Still, I was worried. But there was nothing more I could do. I wrapped my arms around Elisabeth.

She squirmed in my grasp. "Macy," she growled.

I released her and turned towards the steep side of the ditch.

I climbed out of the ditch and started walking down the trail, away from my friend and my sister, and into the darkness.

Time stretched out. I shivered in the warm night and walked faster. Now that I was alone, I jumped at every sound. I wanted to run back to my friends and hide in the ditch till morning.

But then I thought about them. They were alone, in the dark and probably just as scared as I was. Jennica was unconscious and Elisabeth was only nine. They were counting on me. If I went back now, no one would know where we were.

It was up to me. But what if I failed?

"I can't fail." I moaned. Then I thought of Jennica. I took a deep breath and, squaring my shoulders, I spoke into the darkness, "No, I won't fail."

*I am an adventurer*, I thought. "*I will never give up.*" For the first time since the adventure started, I smiled. I walked on, heart pounding, yet determined to get home.

Soon I saw the path that led to our neighborhood.

I ran to the street. In the brightness of a familiar streetlight I suddenly felt exhausted. I could barely keep my eyes open. But the thought of Jennica and Elisabeth gave me the strength to continue. When I got home, several people ran out the door with flashlights.

"Macy," my mom called. Before I knew what was happening, I was being held in her arms. "We were so worried about you."

For a second, I was content to just be held. Then I remembered.

"Mom," I said, pulling free of her gentle embrace. "Elisabeth and Jennica are still on the trail. Jennica's hurt and Elisabeth stayed with her to keep her safe." My mom rushed me inside and sent my dad to search for Jennica and Elisabeth. I sank down into the old armchair in our living room. I knew Jennica and Elisabeth would be safe.

My parents finally came home about three in the morning with Elisabeth. Jennica's concussion turned out to be not too bad and her mom had taken her home.

★ ★ ★

"And that's where my story ends," I say, looking around at my attentive audience, consisting of my brother Tyler, my parents, Jennica's mom, and our pet cat Cup Cake. "I have just one question."

"Ask away, Macy," says my dad.

"How did you know to come home at the exact time we needed you?"

"Well, your brother can answer that best." My dad nods towards Tyler.

"I was in my room when I noticed it was dark. I hadn't heard you knock, so I searched the house. When I didn't find you, I called Mom and Dad." He smiles self-consciously at me. "I could never forget about you and Elisabeth."

My dad raises an eyebrow. "I guess you won't want to ride the Old Kidnapper Trail again for a long time after what happened last night."

"Are you kidding? Of course I do!" I say, to my dad's great astonishment. "After all, I'm an adventurer and adventurers never give up. But next time I'll bring the tools."

# Shadows and the Battle for Omicron

Shadows ran toward his ship as sounds of battle filled the air. *I must get help*, he thought. As he climbed the ladder into his ship, he heard a loud explosion that momentarily drowned out the sounds of battle. Shadows turned around to see someone in the middle of the battlefield, crying as she bent over a limp body of a fallen friend. He looked out past the battle to the vast landscape of the planet Omicron. *How can I leave this place at such a time?* Shadows was snapped out of his thoughts when someone yelled his name. He turned his gaze back to the battle to see a big man pushing his way through the battle to him.

"Where are you going, Shadows?" the man asked in a deep voice.

"Commander, I was j-just going to get help f-from planet Cross Center," Shadows stammered as another bomb exploded.

The commander shook his head.

"Cross Center is too far away. You must fly to Clastol and get help."

Shadows nodded and climbed into the cockpit. He flipped switches and turned dials. Suddenly, the ship's engine roared to life. The ship slowly lifted off the brown muddy surface of Omicron. He cast one last glance at the battle still raging on his home planet. He wondered what would happen to his parents and his older sister Neptune; would they survive until he retrieved help? Then he took a breath and pushed a button labeled "Hyperdrive."

★ ★ ★

On Earth, a boy named Leo stepped off the path and into the forest.

"Leo!" He spun around to see his friend Anna looking angry.

"We aren't supposed to be off the path," she said.

"Don't worry, I know the way back if we get lost," Leo replied.

"Fine. But if we get lost I'll blame you."

Leo shrugged. "Picky, picky." Anna walked next to Leo as they made their way through the snow-covered forest.

"I'm glad your parents let you come here. It's not often we get to see each other."

"They made me come," Leo blurted. Anna stopped, a hurt expression on her face.

"What I mean is, I do want to be with you, it's just I didn't know we were meeting in California!" Leo realized his voice had been rising. Anna lowered her green eyes to the ground.

"I'm sorry," Leo apologized. "I'm just mad because my parents aren't getting along. That's why they sent me here."

"I know it's hard for you and your family. But didn't you want to come at all?"

"Of course I did. I wanted to see you." Leo reached out and stroked Anna's brown hair. "Please forgive me. I didn't mean it."

For a moment there was silence. Presently, Anna stepped forward and embraced Leo in a hug. "I forgive you," she whispered.

They held each other for a minute, then they separated and kept walking. Anna broke the silence. "How's the car that you and your dad are working on?"

"Great," Leo responded, grateful that she changed the subject.

"You're so good at fixing things," Anna said. "Hey, you should—"

Anna stopped abruptly. Snow began to fall in sheets and the wind began to howl.

"Blizzard!" Leo yelled. Just as he spoke, they were caught in the worst of it. Snow whirled around, almost blinding them. Anna grabbed his hand. A gust of wind knocked them off their feet. As Leo looked up, he saw something big and silver coming through the storm straight toward them!

★ ★ ★

Shadows spiraled out of control. He could see nothing through the ship's window to show him where to steer. Outside the ship was a blur of white. His hands were also a blur. He flipped switches, pushed buttons, and turned dials. His heart pounded so hard inside his chest, he thought it would burst.

*I'm going to die.* Without warning, the ship crashed into something hard, throwing him against the front window. Then he drifted into darkness.

★ ★ ★

Shadows woke to the sounds of strange animals. The storm had passed. He sat up and saw an odd-looking animal sitting outside the ship's front window.

"My, what an . . . interesting animal you are," Shadows remarked.

"Let's see," he mumbled, "You have wings. You're red. You have feathers and you whistle."

The creature spread its wings and flew off.

★ ★ ★

Leo and Anna brushed themselves off and noticed a ship that was half-buried in the snow. They slowly circled the ship.

"What would a big toy space ship be doing out here?" Anna asked.

"Big toy space ship!?" said a squeaky voice they didn't recognize.

Leo and Anna froze.

A door in the space ship opened and a figure climbed out. The man-sized alien had dark blue skin, short black hair, and gray eyes. He was wearing brown pants and a dark green t-shirt. A long black tail slowly weaved in the air behind him. A pearl-like ball adorned its pointed end.

"I'll have you know this ship IS real. It was made by a famous ship builder, Deveto Deverage. It is NOT a toy."

Leo could see Anna was shaking with fear.

The alien continued. "You would think that you . . . you . . . things would know that." He paused for a moment. "What are you anyway?"

"What are you?" Anna asked, staring at the alien.

"I am an Omonian. I'm from the planet Omicron. Now tell me, what are you?"

"We're humans," Anna answered. "What are you doing here?"

"It appears my ship is broken. It will not start because important pieces of the engine are damaged."

"Can't you fix your ship?" Leo asked boldly.

"No, because . . . uh . . . I didn't pay attention in ship-repair class."

While the alien talked to Anna, Leo went to look at the ship's engine. The alien and Anna followed him.

"Do you see the problem?" The alien asked.

"No, not yet. This is more advanced than I'm accustomed to," Leo answered. "Hey, we didn't catch your name."

"Oh, I'm Shadows. What are your names?"

"I'm Leo and this is my best friend Anna."

"All right, Leo, Anna. Can you help me fix my ship? I need to get back to my planet fast."

"Why do you need to get back so fast?" Anna asked.

"Because there is a battle raging on my home planet."

Leo looked for the problems with the engine. *Some of the wires snapped. And this canister has a hole in it, making it leak chemicals. I can fix those problems, I hope.* "Hey, Shadows," Leo called.

"Yes?" Shadows, who had been talking with Anna, turned his attention to Leo.

"Do you have some spare wires and some tools?"

"Yes. Do you want them?"

Leo nodded.

"Okay." Shadows ducked into his space ship.

Anna moved closer to Leo, looking worried.

"Something wrong?" he asked, concerned.

"Well, it's just that now we know aliens are real, what if they attack us?"

"Well, if they do, we'll figure something out."

"I wish I could be as optimistic as you," Anna whispered.

Suddenly, Shadows jumped out of the ship. "I've got the supplies," he announced holding a toolbox.

"Great." Leo took the toolbox from Shadows.

"Please hurry. I must get back home soon."

Leo nodded and got to work.

★ ★ ★

"Done!" Leo finally called.

Shadows ran to his ship. "You're good," he said as he looked at the engine.

Anna ran up to them panting, a look of horror on her face.

"What's wrong?" Leo asked her.

Anna was shaking so much, she couldn't speak. She looked to the sky in fear as she pointed.

Leo and Shadows spun around. A terrifying creature flew across the sky. It had the body of a panther, the wings of a raven, and the head of a fox.

"W-what is that?" Leo asked in a hoarse voice.

Shadows knew. "That is a Romegar. They are the enemies that were attacking Omicron."

The creature alighted on Shadows' ship. "Ah, Shadows. I am Screech, and I've been following you since you left the battle. Did you think you could escape death that easily?"

★ ★ ★

Screech jumped straight at them. Leo, Anna, and Shadows scattered. Screech flew after Leo first. Leo ran through the forest until he came to an open field. He looked around for cover. He saw some bushes near a small cave. Leo dashed over and managed to crawl inside.

Roaring in anger, Screech flew off to find someone else. When he got back to the clearing, he saw Anna. She screamed and ran. Screech laughed. *Foolish little creatures. Always running from their problems.*

142

He spread his wings to fly after Anna, but a weight dropped on his back. He roared in anger as it knocked him to the ground. He struggled, but it was too heavy. He passed out.

"Don't move," said Shadows, as Screech regained consciousness.

Screech opened his eyes. A chain was wrapped around his neck and was attached to Shadows' ship.

Shadows stood before Screech. "Now, answer my questions or I'll leave you for the humans," he commanded. "Why are the Romegar attacking Omicron? And why are you trying to kill these innocent humans?" Screech ignored him.

"Answer my questions," Shadows commanded again.

Screech still defied him.

Shadows balled his hands into fists and shook with anger.

Screech grinned evilly. "The Romegar are wise and good fighters. When we win, your people will revere us."

Anger flared in Shadows' eyes like fire.

"One more push should do it," said Screech under his breath. "When we win, your people will wonder why. And the answer is that you didn't get help. The truth is you're a coward."

★ ★ ★

Shadows let his anger erupt. He grabbed a large wrench from the toolbox, and charged at Screech, yelling.

"I'm not a coward!" He let all his anger power him. He lifted the wrench over his head. When he was in range, he swung it at the Romegar's head.

Screech ducked low to the ground and lunged forward. He grabbed Shadows' legs and knocked him down.

Shadows landed on his back with a dull thud, stunned. Pain erupted in his right leg. He rolled on his side in an attempt to get back up. But as he rolled, hot spikes shot into his tail. He yowled and looked back to see Screech's claws gripping his tail. Before Shadows could react, Screech pinned him to the ground.

"Say your prayers," Screech hissed. He raised his other claw to strike. "Because they will be your last."

★ ★ ★

Anna sprinted through the woods. Her heart pounded in her chest. *Must find Leo! Must find Leo!*

She rounded a huge tree trunk and ran straight into Leo. He tumbled to the ground.

143

"Leo! We must get back to the ship and help Shadows. He has Screech pinned down. But Screech won't stay down for long."

Leo jumped to his feet and shook snow off his coat. "Lead the way."

Anna nodded and took off running. As the two neared the clearing, they heard a yell. Anna put on a burst of speed. Screech was poised above Shadows to deliver a death blow.

"No!" Anna shouted. Screech looked up.

He crackled. "Say goodbye to your friend. You're next."

★ ★ ★

Leo bolted forward. He grabbed a big stick and leaped onto Screech's back. He brought it down with all his might onto Screech's neck. Screech roared and loosed his grip, allowing Shadows to wiggle away. Shadows charged toward his ship and scrambled in, only to reemerge again with a small green space gun.

"Leo, get off him!" Shadows shouted.

Leo jumped off Screech and ran to Shadows' side. Anna ran from the trees to them. Shadows held up the gun and took aim. "Stay back," he ordered Leo and Anna.

Shadows pointed the gun at Screech's shoulder and fired. The projectile hit and burst open, covering Screech in green liquid. The monster roared in anger as the liquid spread over his entire body. When the liquid had covered his body completely, it started glowing. Slowly, Screech started fading.

"This isn't the last you've seen of me! I'll be back!" he roared as he disappeared.

Leo and Anna stared at Shadows.

"I never thought I'd have to use this," Shadows said, looking sadly at the gun in his hands.

Leo shook himself. "At least you saved us," he said.

Shadows looked at the sky. "I should go now that my ship is fixed." Shadows turned toward his ship.

"Wait!" Anna called. "Is there any way we can stay in contact? I mean, it's not every day you meet a friendly alien."

Shadows smiled. He reached into his pocket and drew out two small devices. He handed them each one. "You speak into it," he instructed. "Then to send your message, press the center button."

"Thanks." Anna said.

Shadows gave one last nod and ran to his ship. He dragged the ladder in and shut the door. Leo and Anna waved as the ship lifted up into the darkened sky. Leo squinted. Shadows waved back, just before his ship flew off into outer space.

"We should go back to the campsite," Leo announced.

"Let's," Anna agreed and took his hand.

★ ★ ★

Two days later, Leo awoke to a strange buzzing sound. He sat up in bed and rubbed sleep out of his eyes. He looked around for the source of the noise. Finally, his gaze came to rest upon his desk. The device Shadows had given him two days before was shaking. Leo jumped out of bed, ran over, and picked it up. The buzzing stopped and words appeared on the small square screen. He read them out loud.

> "Leo, thanks to your engineering
> skills and your quick thinking,
> we won the battle!—Shadows"

Leo sat down in his desk chair and spoke into the device.

> "No problem. It was easy fixing
> your big toy space ship.—Leo"

He smiled and then pressed the button labeled "Send."

*Juvenile Bald Eagle On His Way*, Fairl Thomas

# Genesis

This queer boy's body has been alienating me from its conception
but never so much as at 15 years old.
That's when I became a statistic.
Not the 1 in 4 women sexually assaulted.
Not the 1 in 16 men.
I AM THE 47% OF TRANSGENDER PEOPLE RAPED IN THEIR
LIFETIME.
Stuck in-between,
trying to claim an experience that I was never sure was mine,
trying to justify
or explain
or validate
my survivorship
hoping someone
anyone
would believe me.
But they don't need to believe me.
The truth does not change with the words I speak,
it is not my obligation to convince others that my rape is legitimate.
This is my healing story, and it is not contingent on anyone's approval.
This is my survivorship
this is my recovery
this is my journey.
This is the story that matters:
I AM A QUEER MALE ASSAULT SURVIVOR.
They don't tell you that not all rape is
back-alley shadows
drunken parties
strangers who stalk you home.
Rape is a friend
a family member
a lover.
But I am more than what he took
and took

and took.
That is not the story, only a footnote.
It is only one of thousands of origins and it is not this narrator's sole plot point.
He is not responsible for my tenderness
my queerness
my sweetness
my manhood.
I am not what I am because of him but rather in spite
and it is in spite that I speak
dance
write
LIVE.
Because this world needs better people.
This world needs better men.
I have seen them
and I will be them.
So I'm practicing gentleness
kindness
forgiveness.
If others deserve it, so do I.
A fear that he raped someone after me is not a weight I can hold.
So I've had to let it go;
am still learning how.
I want other assault survivors to know:
this is not the end.
It is a Genesis.

# Old News

After the funeral, the estate lawyer had given Caroline an envelope addressed to her in her mother's handwriting. Inside the envelope she found her father's address and a photograph. Caroline had never met her father. She stared at the address with the same mixture of disdain and curiosity that she'd felt whenever she thought about him. It wasn't that Caroline felt rejected by him. Her mother, Lisa, had made it clear that her father hadn't abandoned Caroline; he didn't know about her. Since he'd abruptly broken up with Lisa, she'd never told him. Although Lisa seemed to have forgiven him, she discouraged Caroline's questions about him, answering them briefly and then changing the subject. Caroline had never tried to find him. She was disgusted with the way he'd treated her mother. But after her mother died, that feeling was swallowed by the hole that grief had dug inside her, and curiosity won. As Caroline studied her father's picture in her hand, her pulse quickened. It was unsettling to see her own eyes looking back at her from the gaze of someone from whom she'd felt so distant. Soon she'd be meeting him at the café for the first time.

Dan awakened that morning, taking longer than usual to orient himself. *Today's the day.* He was so anxious that his eyes raced around the room as though seeking somewhere to focus their energy, but his legs insisted on staying under the covers. Finally, his curiosity and desire to meet his daughter pushed him out of bed. While he dressed, Dan reflected on that shadowy period, twenty-three years ago. He'd been told he had Huntington's disease. The diagnosis changed his entire world. He felt out of control, angry, as if he were someone else. Before he got sick, he and Lisa had planned to travel the world, getting odd jobs and apartments wherever. He didn't want pity and wanted Lisa to have the free, adventurous life they'd planned. So he broke up with her without explanation. He'd watched her eyes widen with shock and well up with tears, but she wasn't the type of person to beg for answers when

149

faced with rejection. She stormed out before the first tear rolled down her cheek. He could still hear the door slamming between them. It turned out the doctor had been wrong, but Dan never contacted Lisa. He didn't understand how he could have acted the way he did. He couldn't reconcile the fool he'd been with the person he needed to see himself as. Besides, there was no point disrupting her life again. She'd likely met someone else. Now, after all these years, even though he'd been estranged from Lisa, it seemed impossible that she was gone. He couldn't believe that he was getting a second chance at a connection with Lisa through Caroline. He wondered if he'd glimpse Lisa in Caroline—and a reflection of his history floating on this new face.

Dan sat at a table in front with his cup of black coffee, and tried to prepare himself. He still liked to start his day with the paper rather than getting his news online. His colleagues teased him about being old school, but he was a history teacher after all. He sought comfort in its cool, crinkly pages, the predictability of it being part of his morning ritual. He attempted to read, but as he thumbed through his thoughts, excitement turned to angst. His stomach turned along with them. Since Caroline hadn't sent him her picture, or even told him that she had hazel eyes just like his, he searched for the only familiarity he could imagine. He scanned faces for traces of Lisa.

At a table in back, Caroline sipped chamomile tea. Its flowery warmth steadied her breath. Since he had no idea what she looked like, she had the upper hand. Of course that also meant she'd have to approach him. What if he was the jerk she'd always feared he was? Or just weird? The shadow of disloyalty darkened over her, as though she were betraying her mother by seeking him out after what he'd done to her mother. On her wrist, a heart dangled from the silver charm bracelet that had been her mother's. She ran her fingers over its rounded top. *No, if mom had been against me meeting him, she wouldn't have made sure I had his address and photo.* Hoping to muster her mother's courage, she squeezed the silver heart charm.

If only Dan had known about Caroline back then. He wondered how he could explain now. Caroline wouldn't understand that after he'd learned he wasn't sick, he'd been too ashamed and filled with regret about how he'd handled things to tell her mother the truth. In the light

150

of the café, amid aromas of bacon and toast, the voices of strangers, it all seemed so lame. Dan buried his face in his hands. *I can't do this. I'm not ready.*

Caroline knew that meeting him might be awkward, but she figured, *how bad could it be? If it doesn't go well I'll just go back to not having a father.* She stood. *Now or never.* The silver heart clanked as it hit the back of her chair. Unseen by Dan, Caroline walked slowly toward him.

Dan tried the breathing exercises he'd learned to cope with anxiety—in for a count of four, hold for seven, exhale for eight. Still, panic pushed him out of his chair. Once again, he couldn't own his choices. He feared he'd only disappoint Caroline. Dan bolted, leaving his paper—soon to be tossed into the trash as yesterday's news with coffee grounds and bagel crumbs.

*He's leaving? No way.* Caroline rushed toward him. His hand was on the door. She wished he would turn around. Caroline fumed. Just as she was about to call out to him, she stopped herself. *What's his excuse this time?* Of course he didn't have one when he'd left her mom either. *He's pitiful. Mom was right to have let him go. We were better off without him.* A gust of cold air swept in, chilling Caroline as the door slammed between them. Her water-blurred hazel eyes watched history repeat itself.

She picked up the newspaper he left behind—filled with facts and stories, all told from a chosen angle, in black and white, on finger-smudged, wilting pages agape and hanging off the plastic red table. Could there have been more to the story than what her mother had told her?

Outside, the window reflected Dan's empty chair. His legs cast shadows on the sidewalk.

Inside, Caroline stirred her second cup of tea. *Things might have been different if only mom had told him about me in the beginning.* She tensed. Then, fidgeting with the heart on her mother's charm bracelet, tracing its point at the bottom, she felt the sting of guilt. How could she fault her mother? Was he giving up on her the same way he'd given up on his relationship with her mother?

*But he doesn't even know me.* In a way, her mother had given up on her father too. Even though she didn't know what made him leave today, he must have wanted to meet her, or he wouldn't have come. He was the only close family she had. Going forward, Caroline decided to change this family trend of giving up.

Outside in the brisk air, Dan's heart stopped pounding. His muscles relaxed. The sense of relief made him feel that he'd been right to leave the cafe. But as soon as that feeling unfolded, he realized it was the same false satisfaction he'd experienced when he managed to put off some task he really wanted done, but couldn't bear to do. *Here I go again, running away.* He felt a sharp pain in his side. Rallying his defenses, he reminded himself that he liked life the way it was. He enjoyed his career—his research and colleagues. He couldn't hold on to any of his thoughts. One ricocheted off the other till their points were just arrows, piercing his momentary resolve, whizzing through him. He needed to put the whole fiasco with Lisa behind him. *Everything to do with Lisa is the past—even Caroline. She's a grown woman. She doesn't need me.* He thought again about how happy teaching made him. The students were the best part. *Caroline would be the same age.* Dan's pace slowed as he wondered if she liked history, imagined the conversations they might have. But how could he overcome his fear? He didn't have any history of success in that area to guide him. A girl about five or six years old brushed past him and smiled. The next thing he knew, Dan pivoted and walked back toward the café. Dan had been so anxious, he'd gotten to the café much too early before, so if he hurried, Caroline might still be there.

While Dan was turning the corner, the door clanged behind Caroline walking in the opposite direction. She had turned a page in her own history. Though the wind stung her eyes, she felt as though a ray of sun shining in the attic was burning through dust on a locked box she'd thought she would never want to open. Its illuminated key now drew her like a magnet.

Dan couldn't believe he'd made it back to the café. Drumming his fingers on the edge of his seat, he wondered if he'd stay this time.

Bitterness, guilt, rejection and loss had whipped themselves up inside Caroline like a frozen macchiato. Now that it was beginning to settle, something like hope seemed to be rising to the top. After coming this far, she would not give up on meeting him. Just a short while ago she was alone, but now she had seen him, been just feet away from him, watched his expressions, his movements. Now, he was real. She buttoned her coat against the blustery day, determined to find her way.

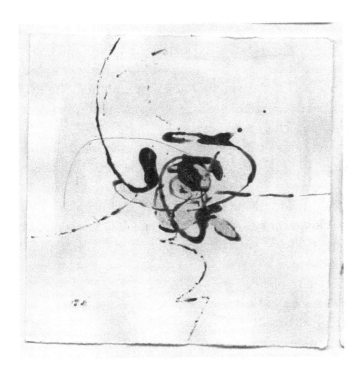

# One-Way Street

He wore a ruby bow tie and polka dot suspenders. Clutching a bouquet of wild flowers, his derby hat tilted a little to the left, he stood at her door waiting for the chimes to finish their musical prelude. His heart beat a little faster. The door slowly opened and their eyes met, as they had countless times during the long history of their friendship. Deceased spouses. Growing families. Life and social circles.

"Hello, Blanche!" he choked, finding his square dance caller voice. "I've dreamed of this moment for the last thirty years and now I'm here. Finally here. Will you go out for dinner with me?"

One month later, Grandma was announcing her engagement to Gene Clawson. This news was not received well from a room full of astonished children. Grown children . . . who were absolutely content in the knowledge that Blanche was ONLY their mother and grandmother. She triumphantly held up her left hand, revealing the tiniest engagement ring like it was a prize. Everyone silently shifted in their seats.

What would this mean for all of us? Would Grandma still cook dinner on Thanksgiving? Would she still do her crafts with us? Crochet lessons hung in the balance.

"How can she do this to us?!" Dad shouted from the driver seat on the way home. We kids shrunk down lower, green LTD leather grabbing our skin. "This Gene Clawson will take our inheritance! This is BULLSHIT!"

Tense holidays.

Heartbreaking silences.

A different man in Grandpa's chair.

Everything changed.

Dad didn't like change.

But Blanche, my grandma, was also changed. She smiled now, giggled when Gene came up behind her at the stove. Flowers appeared on the table. He winked at her, always wearing a bow tie for dinner. They held hands and had conversations in hushed tones. He kissed her and hugged her. They belonged together despite the fact that the family was pissed.

Years passed, and I watched the changes in everyone and saw how he was the same to Grandma. He was what she deserved and needed. And he was the grandfather I needed. He came to my dance recitals and always smiled at me with a wink. He went to my high school classroom and read "Paul Revere's Ride" with a fierce thundering voice. He was perfect. I saw what she saw. He was real despite what Dad thought about him.

When Grandma got sick, Gene was there every day . . . sometimes all night. When she thought she was riding a Ferris wheel, he calmly explained about the hospital bed and how she was perfectly normal. He even pretended to climb down off the perceived apparatus.

When she eventually passed, Gene sat beside her coffin leaning on his cane. All alone, the family ignoring him. I sat down beside him and leaned in. He reciprocated.

I noticed he had her rings in his hand. A tear fell and he said, "She was a good wife."

"And you were a wonderful husband," I replied.

It was a moment—a moment where you can see the path clearly. A moment when you understand things on new levels.

"Gene?"

"Yes, Janet?"

"I love you."

"Well," he replied in a hushed voice. "You're not on a one-way street."

# Night Crawlers

Jimmy came out of the side door
    real slow, catchin' the screen door
        softly, with a raised knee, just
            before it woulda hit and rattled, he was
                bein' extra careful
                not to make any sudden noises,
        wakin' up Ma
    or the henhouse chickens.
Now, Jimmy wasn't supposed to hang out
with us trouble kids no more,
    after the incident with Old Man Perkins'
        yard, they call it "The Incident"
            like it was some big deal or somethin'
                when he caught us, the whole bunch of
                us, eatin' melons and such, we were just
        havin' some fun, now . . .
    in the fields . . .
and Old Man Perkins,
he raised such a stinkin' fuss
    —even if he had hundreds of juicy, drippy, red, ready ripe ones.
        Makes your mouth salivate,
        uncontrollably,
        just thinkin' 'bout
        just even thinkin' 'bout those beautiful treats straight from
    God's green earth
and, how's he gonna miss a few
    now and then? You tell me.
        'Cause I just don't know what all
            the hootin' and hollerin' was all about
                and half of them probably just go to rot in this
            hot, shiny sun, anyways.
        How many melons can you possibly sell out of your old
    pickup truck at Fast Elmer's Fillin' Station
that gets no customers?

# ODET

Well, hardly any compared to the way it was before,
    after they put the big road bypass
and nobody even comes through our lost-the-factory dyin' town anyways.

So, Jimmy comes out of the kitchen side,
    tippy toein' and shushin' all of us.

        Why?

I don't know. 'Cause we're all self-shushin' anyhow.

We know the drill, and, we were barely whisperin' mostly,
    and, we keep it that way till we make it clean out
        past the fence by Bingham Road.

We call it Bing, Bing, Bingham Road
        'cause it's funny.

Now it's just what we call it . . .
    takin' no chances 'cause we're gonna figure out
        what's goin' on
    near behind Grandma Malone's used-to-be-farm and pasture land
    and what not but now it's all private and choppy fenced and such.
But we see comin's and goin's
        and the whole town don't notice but us,
'cause it's way out where,
        not between spots no more
      and, we crawled and climbed, looked and searched.
    There wasn't nothin' there
but we expected somethin', you know.

We had high expectations that somethin' special—real interestin' and weird
      and private
      and questionable
was happenin' out there at Grandma Malone's used-to-be place.

Then Pete and Eugene, well, they took notice of a crinkly kinda sound.

They rousted us to go check it out, investigate what it was,
spy-like,
and after a bit, we saw a dim light glow way out there by the
back barn and our imaginations, well, we just knew that it was some
secret government installation with UFOs and radioactive emissions and men
in Hazmat suit-type attire. Probably chemists and scientists, you know,
lookin' at isotopes and oscilloscopes, microscopes, and telescopes and the
multiple antenna type of head protrusions on those little green critter
beings from Jupiter and Neptune and some of Saturn's rings that you know
are just space colony moons.

Eugene and Bo, well, they think that those space type critters don't have
regular kinda teeth, that frogs and lizards and such, live in their mouths
and catch and partially digest the food and bugs and flies for their
particular host being overlords,
and regurgitate
the semi-processed,
stinky like a dead dog, hit by a truck in the middle of the road last week
but now it's on the side of the road 'cause your dad was kind enough
to shovel it over to the edge 'cause he didn't want to run over that
same hound's remains every time he went that road
and stunk up his truck real bad every damn time.

That stuff gets old fast, he says.

Well, we crawled and climbed, tippy-toed and snuck over to peer
over the boards and scrap metal leanings pile
—knowin' and expectin'—
all of us—a crazy weird scene.

Somethin' strange was going on and we were just about to discover
and uncover it all
and it turned out real disappointin' bad.
Jimmy's dad and some other guys were just gathered 'round a burn barrel
drinkin' and who knows what

and then he spotted us, and began to cuss,
tellin' us to get the hell in the back of the darn
truck.

Let's go home, dammit. And don't you even think about tellin' your mama
what you seen out here.
Or anyone else.
You just keep your mouths shut. About what you seen
or heard or smelt out here.
It ain't nobody's business what goes on out here. You
don't say nothin'.
You hear?

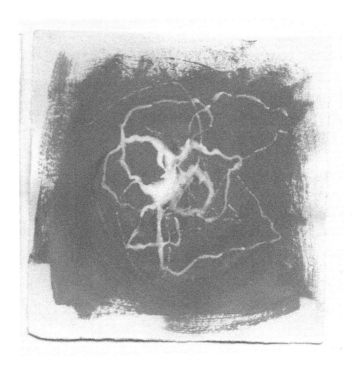

Roger Howard

# Black Lined Roads

I follow dirt roads in the evening,
twisty black lines on a map,
borders stretching to the underbrush,
long buried tree trunks,
a crude foundation bed.

Shadows pushing into the distance,
lengthening as the sun sets,
the muted sounds of the coming evening
a whispered cacophony for the senses,
an unspoiled symphony of dusk.

I've seen dirt roads at the end of sunlight,
so quiet you can hear your heart.
Black lines on a map,
in the growing shadows,
comforting for those traveling light.

I follow dirt roads in the evening,
twisty black lines on a map.
Stretching like an indolent serpent.
Those black lines are calling.
Dirt roads are waiting,

waiting for me.

# The Last Train Out

It was not big news in the local paper. How could it be these days, when so many world events were on people's minds? A small item in the second section merely mentioned the event. The front section was occupied with the present and preoccupied about the future. News of then-Congo, atomic bombs, the United Nations, and the space race predominated.

Statements and speeches by assorted statesmen dealt with the many dangers lurking about, threatening world peace. And, of course, the analysts and pundits were having their say. They were wont to believe that the problems of the world could be magically resolved with a few nice words and a well-turned phrase.

Sunday evening at 7:10, according to the paper, would mark the last time a steam engine would pull a train out of town. My wife and our two boys came to say goodbye and to take a last look, for to us it was more than the end of another era; it was the closing of so many pleasant memories. Since our eldest boy had learned to talk, we had come here to show him the big engine that made all that noise, whose every movement was fascinating, even in the eyes of one so young. Here he expressed so many facets of his young personality—curiosity, joy, and fear. In later years, his younger brother joined him.

There were not too many people on the platform, but at one time or another, when we had stood at this station, we had seen most of these faces before. There was old Jos Barril. He was 81 and stood straight with eyes so bright and sharp that no movement nor details were missed. We had become well acquainted with Jos, and the children loved him for the many railroad stories he had told them. His life in railroading started when he was 16. At that time, the railroad was just coming into town, and he was hired to lay the tracks down and to swing the big sledgehammer that drove the dog spikes, which held them on the sleepers.

The children were running up and down the platform, climbing the trucks that took the mail, luggage, and freight on and off the train. They were looking at the blackboard that was nailed onto the station wall, trying to decipher the names and numbers printed on it.

In the distance, we could see it coming now. Proud as ever, its smoke clinging close by a breeze, helping her to avoid any last-minute criticism from her ejected soot. She was approaching unaware of her fate, undaunted by the present, unmindful of her past. Somehow, through our misty eyes, she looked different today. She seemed old and tired, even weak as she finally came to a stop. We gathered around her and just looked silently, each of us in his own mind, attempting to capture a final memory or a pleasure evoked from the past.

My cherished memories of the old steam engine were from the years on the farm, as a boy, where the railroad passed directly through the middle of the pasture. It reminded me of the many days and summers when, after gathering the cows from the pasture to the fence, I would sit on top of a post and wait for the 4:50 p.m. to pass before I would let the cows cross on their way to be milked. She would come around the curve way past Lowe's farm, right at the foot of the majestic Laurentian Mountains, her smoke billowing in the air. When she drew close to the Fifth Concession crossing, her whistle, sharp and loud, would warn the road travelers of her imminent approach. She would roar by like a racer with her arms close to her body, rotating the big steel wheels as they creaked along the track. Oh, how many times I had wished I could be aboard that big engine, traveling at great speeds across the country . . .

I was brought out of my reverie by Jos's unusual movement at this time. He pulled his railway watch from his vest pocket and said, "She's on time. She's still faithful after all these years." To Jos Barril, it meant so much. He had been with the railroad for 50 years when he retired. The steam engine had given him a good income throughout his life, besides the pleasure, adventures, and memories. He had loved that life and never had any complaints about any part of it. Old Jos knew the railroad business inside and out. He was a legend in the district for the facts and details he could give about railroading. A description of any type of engine, its wheel arrangement, and even its tractive effort in pounds, could be supplied from memory at any time from Jos. The water, coal, or fuel capacities of any tenders were other references obtainable from him. There was an air of mystery when he mentioned the International, the Dominion, the Alouette, the Winnipegger, or any other trains. Along with this, he could give you their routes, the distance covered, the booked time, the average load and speed of each. Where or when these engines were built, the seating accommodations of first class coaches, or the numbers of sections in the sleeping car were kept in his mind, as if on file.

If you cared about freight equipment, Jos would rattle off the sizes and capacities of the flat, box, coal, tank, refrigerator or any other cars used. Nobody ever doubted him, whether he talked about the 32-mile Aroostook Valley and the 3,223-mile Minneapolis-St. Paul run by C.P. in the U.S.A., or the highest altitude (3.717 feet) reached by rail in Canada at Yellowhead, British Columbia.

He had held many jobs on the train and steam engine, starting as a fireman and retiring as a conductor. From these different jobs, Jos had acquired the knowledge of all the codes, symbols, and signals of the railways, and the meaning of the track and yard standards.

He would readily admit that the steam engine had faults, that she had dirtied many a washing hung on the clothes lines as soot poured out of her when she struggled to pull a heavy freight train. Jos would also grant that the cities and the areas surrounding the stations were dirty. He even admitted that she was late at times. But he had many answers in her favor. When you love, the faults are light on your heart and easily minimized by the good points. All you had to do was look at the service this steam engine had rendered in the rain, the cold, and the storms. Her faults were outweighed by the joys of happy reunions of families and friends on the station platforms, the jobs she had created, and the opportunities and services she delivered to all industries. The agricultural, mining, and forest industries were particularly aided by her.

Two short sounds on the train's communicating signals indicated that she was ready to leave for the last time. Old Jos pulled his watch from his vest pocket but, without looking at it, slipped it back again. She released a jet of steam, and small white puffs came out of her stack, increasing in sound and darkening in color until it became so powerful that the soot was pouring all over us. The big steel wheels started to turn slowly, pulled by the strong arms at her side. Edging gently at first, she then hurriedly pulled away like a lover tearing herself away from the one she loves.

Old Jos took a few steps forward, pulled his polka-dotted handkerchief from his back pocket, wiped his eyes, and watched the last train out.

*Longyearbyen, Svalbard, 78° N,* Warren Firschein

# CONTRIBUTORS

**W. S. Ahlen** is the pen name of Gary Hogenson whose stories have appeared in previous *Odet* editions. In the search for the pathway between points A and B he turned to poetry to express the eternal nature of being; that the outcome of the journey changes by the very act of going from one place to the next. A retired engineer and financial executive, his career centered on numbers and formulas, not words. He discovered writing four years ago when he joined the Tarpon Springs Writer's Group.

**Gerri Almand**'s works have appeared in *The Florida Writer, Orchids: The Bulletin of the AOS, The Sun, Odet, The Tampa Bay Sounding,* and *Wanderlust.* Her debut nonfiction book, *The Reluctant RV Wife,* was released in 2019. With a permanent address in Tampa, Gerri and her husband now trade reluctancies. She continues to feel quasi-reluctant on the road and he feels acutely-reluctant at home.

**Abigail Anderson** is a creative fiction writer and not an astronaut, but that doesn't stop her from writing about aliens and space adventures. From a fierce rabbit who eats coloring-books to her six strange siblings, Abigail has plenty of source material for out-of-this-world adventures.

**Alatheia Anderson** loves to bike with her best friend and her sister. She also loves to write in her room with her paper-eating bunny. She goes on all kinds of amazing, yet crazy adventures with her family. When Alatheia is not writing or keeping her rabbit from eating something, she likes to relax and draw.

**Sami Andrews** is a 16-year-old aspiring young writer and artist who is homeschooled. Her first ever published story was featured in *Odet* in 2019. Sami loves to sketch and watercolor paint, listen to music, play flag-football and other sports, coach gymnastics, and hang out with her brother and friends.

**Holly Apperson** has lived in the Tampa Bay area since birth. She began learning photography in high school and hasn't been able to put her camera down since. Her Nikon helps capture her beautiful surroundings but she enjoys exploring other subject matters as well. Her work has been published in corporate publications and promotions, and in *A Brief History of Safety Harbor, Florida* and *Odet.*

**Roy Ault** was a teacher, coach and administrator in the public schools and universities of Ohio for many years. In 1971 he resigned from the education field and went into business. That business continues today with son, Brad, as president. Roy and wife, Sherrie, moved to Englewood, Florida in 1979. In 1986, Roy became a columnist for the *Charlotte Sun,* a daily newspaper serving Charlotte, Lee, DeSoto and Sarasota Counties. Roy has a Master's Degree in Education, a wife of 63 years and a daughter, Misty, who teaches high school chemistry, physics and anatomy. Roy is grandfather to three wonderful grandsons.

**Mary Bast,** senior editor of *Bacopa Literary Review,* has published poetry, found poetry, and creative nonfiction in a variety of print and online journals. Recently retired from her career as an Enneagram mentor/coach, she's authored or co-authored five professional Enneagram books. Mary is also an award-winning artist and a board member of the Gainesville Fine Arts Association.

**Patricia Blauvelt** creates her art as a personal journey to encourage the viewer to cherish the nature around us. She often uses macro photography and abstract images because the process is meditative, requiring patience, time, and a real connection to the smallest details surrounding her. It is, as well, a challenge in her study of light and shadows, lines, and color. Her artistic goal is to share this beauty. She is active in exhibits in the Tampa Bay area, where she has lived since 1985.

**Kahlia Bouler** is 12-years old and lives in Tampa with her family. She likes writing and basketball. She writes based off of the things she sees around her. She started writing at the age of six but noticed she had a gift at the age of 11. The goal of her writing is to be a voice calling out injustice against humans.

**Kevan Breitinger** is a working mosaic artist from St. Augustine who loves words so much she uses them in her message-driven art as well. She has lived in Florida for ten years now and says that moving here to a land of breathtaking beauty was the wisest thing she has ever done for herself.

**Aramis Calderon** earned his MFA in Creative Writing from the University of Tampa. Every week he participates in the DD-214 Writers' Workshop, a writing community for active duty service members, veterans, and their families. He currently resides in Safety Harbor, Florida with his wife and three children.

**Crystel Calderon**'s entry in the 2016 Safety Harbor Library's Six Word Memoir Contest won first place. Crystel is a lover of books and art and has degrees to match her passions. She dreams of opening a book store one day.

**April Carter** is studying English Education and writing studies at the University of South Florida's St. Petersburg campus. She is President of USFSP's chapter of Sigma Tau Delta English Honor Society and editor of *Papercut,* USFSP's literary journal. April plans to continue her education by pursuing her Master's degree in English Education. She hopes to teach ELA at the high school or college level upon completing her degree. In her free time, you can find her with her head stuck in a book or creating poems or stories of her own.

**Chelsea Catherine** is a PEN Short Story Prize Nominee, winner of the Raymond Carver Fiction contest in 2016, a Sterling Watson fellow, and an Ann McKee grant recipient. Her novella, "Blindsided" won the Clay Reynolds competition and was published in October of 2018. Most recently, she won the Mary C Mohr nonfiction award through the Southern Indiana Review and her book, *Summer of the Cicadas,* won the Quill Prose Award through Red Hen Press. It will be published in 2020.

**George Chase** studied art at Ringling College of Design in Sarasota, Florida and Art Center College of Design in Los Angeles. He worked as an art director at Leo Burnett, USA in Chicago, creating TV and print ads before establishing his graphic design business, Chase Creative. His art has been used to illustrate books, events, locales, religious figures and more. His work has won over thirty national design awards.

**Eileen Vorbach Collins** lives in Rotonda West, Florida. A member of the Suncoast Writer's Guild she is working on a collection of essays and seldom writes poetry. When she saw a news clip of a mother of one of the Parkland victims, she knew that the reality had not hit and her heart ached for this unfathomable loss.

**Tom Cosentino** is a resident of Indian Rocks Beach and Tarrytown, NY. He has been a member of Safety Harbor Writers & Poets for the last five years. Tom has a BA in Political Science from Syracuse University and an MBA from the Rochester Institute of Technology. He served in the United States Army as a Field Artillery Officer. He has been married to his wife Caye for 30 years and they have two children, Genevieve and Dominic.

**Caitlin Coutant** moved to St. Petersburg, Florida to pursue a BFA in Creative Writing and a BA in Literature from Eckerd College. She often writes fiction based on Florida Man headlines and nonfiction, travel inspired pieces as well. Following her graduation, she plans to stay in Florida where her fifty-five orchids are much happier than they were in childhood hometown in upstate New York.

**L. H. Davis'** post-apocalyptic short story, "Shoot Him Daddy," was published in Metasaga's anthology, *Futuristica Vol. 1* in 2016. "That Last Summer," a short, young-adult work, was published in *Red Truck Review*'s third literary journal in 2015. He won the 2018 Teleport Science Fiction Contest with his short story "Domain of the Dragon." *Dreaming Robot Press* recently selected his short story, "Girl Meets Robot," for inclusion in their *Young Explorer's Adventure Guide, Volume 6*.

**Ed Derkevics** lived on Long Island and worked for the USPS. He moved to Florida in 1986 and after several years, discovered a love of writing. Today, he is a folk artist and poet who sells real estate to fortify his love of travel. He hosts a popular open mic called SHAMc Alive at the Safety Harbor Art & Music Center as well as a typewriting event called Quorum of Parrots, where participants can write using Ed's 19 vintage typewriters.

**Jarine Dotson** is a Safety Harbor resident and loves getting up for an early morning walk. Most mornings you'll find her down at the Waterfront Park taking pictures of the sunrise, among other things Safety Harbor. Jarine is a photographic contributor to the *Safety Harbor Sun*, and past editions of *Odet*.

**W. Chris Dotson** is a Safety Harbor resident, and specializes in mixed media. He often uses wood scraps he finds around town, and repurposes them into works of art. More of his work can be found on the Safety Harbor Art Walk, the Sunday Market, or his private studio by appointment. Chris and his wife Jarine were voted "People's

Favorite" at the Safety Harbor Fine Art and Seafood Festival. He is a past contributor to *Odet*.

**Arthur Doweyko** writes science fiction and fantasy. As a PhD scientist, he invented novel drug design software and shares the 2008 Thomas Alva Edison Patent Award for the discovery of Sprycel, an anti-cancer drug. Novels: *Algorithm* (2010 RPLA) and *As Wings Unfurl* (Best Pre-Pub Sci-Fi 2014 RPLA); Anthology: *My Shorts* (13 short stories, pub 2017). Many of his short stories have garnered awards, including Honorable Mentions in the L. Ron Hubbard Writers of the Future Competition. He is also an artist (oil and graphics) who has published book covers and internal illustrations.

**Louise Eastin** who has achieved success in mathematics and computer science as well as poetry, sees poetry as both mirror and magnifying glass, believes poets and readers of poetry venture inside timelines, connect past and future and live more fully in the present. A good poem will return and haunt. During her short time as a submitting poet she has three journal publications and several local, national and international awards, most recently, April 2019, 1st place in the free form poetry division of an International writing competition. She has lived and worked in Ohio and Nebraska, as well as Paris, Exeter (UK), Madrid and Prague, and since 2008 considers Florida her home.

**Bob Ellis** is a retired financial services exec now residing full-time in SW Florida. As a person who has lived on three continents, traveled the world, and swam in all the oceans, he is very familiar with this year's theme. Several of his short fiction pieces, many of which use the world of banking as a backdrop, have been published in collections.

**Warren Firschein** is the co-founder and Managing Editor of *Odet*. He considers the opportunity to work with so many talented writers, poets, artists, and editors over the past four years to be one of the highlights of his writing career, and wishes all of you his best as each of you progress along your own personal journey, no matter where it takes you. He looks forward to reading—and seeing—your future works.

**Dianna Graveman** is a former teacher and college instructor. Originally from Missouri, Dianna became a full-time Florida resident in 2016 and currently works as an editor and freelance writer. She is the author of several published stories and articles and the coauthor of five regional histories.

**Kelley Hails** is a physician, writer, painter, poet, and mindfulness coach. Her poetry comes out of a meditative experience of communion with nature on themes of importance in her life.

**Pat Hambrick** earned her Bachelor of Arts degree in English from the University of AR at Little Rock, She was a journalist and won awards for her writing, then spent several years as a community coalition coordinator. She is a beginning artist (acrylics) and recently began writing again after a long hiatus. Pat lives in the Tampa Bay area.

**Alyssa Harmon** graduated from the University of South Florida, St. Petersburg with a major in English Writing studies. She has several poems published in journals and magazines including *Odet* (Vol. 3), *30 N*, *Minerva Rising*, *Merrimack Review*, and *Cipher*. Eventually, she hopes to publish a collection of her poetry and photography. She enjoys swimming, photography, writing, and watching Marvel movies.

**Roger Howard** was a surgeon and hospital administrator from Michigan who had retired to Clearwater where he focused on perfecting the art of writing poetry. Roger loved being a part of the local writing community and had joined Safety Harbor Writers & Poets where he participated in open mics and classes. He found success in publishing through the *Esthetic Apostle* and this journal. He left a legacy of insight through two books of poetry. Prior to his death in 2018, Roger asked to sponsor a poetry contest, which we called the Roger Howard Poetry Prize. We know he would have been thrilled to read not only the winners' poems, but also all of the works throughout this volume.

**Maureen Jenkins** holds a BA degree from the University of Pittsburgh. She is a playwright and has had many readings and productions of her ten-minute and full-length plays in the United States. Besides playwriting, she is a published poet and a member of the Poets Circle at OLLI. She is a member of the Dramatists Guild, Pinellas County Writers and Suncoast Playwrights. Maureen lives in Pittsburgh in the summer months and Largo, Florida in the winter.

**Karen Koven** is a writer and speaker living in Clearwater. She was awarded first place in the Romeo Lemay Contest, 2018 and has been published in *Odet*, 2018 and 2019. Prior to retirement she was a Senior Consultant with an International Training and Development Company. She has earned Toastmasters International's highest designation, Distinguished Toastmaster. Karen has been a year-round resident of Florida since 1989.

A graduate of Mississippi College, **Amy Lauren** was a finalist for the 2019 Tennessee Williams Poetry Prize. Her chapbooks include *Prodigal*, *God With Us*, and *She/Her/Hers*. She has published in *The Gay & Lesbian Review*, *Cordite Poetry Review*, *New Orleans Review*, and elsewhere.

**Janet Lee** is a media producer, instructional Designer, and author living in Safety Harbor since 2014. She is active in the art community and is often involved in local events, parades, and good will projects. She loves to walk at the Safety Harbor marina with her two golden doodle dogs, Charlee and William.

**Romeo Lemay** was born in Quebec, Canada in 1924 and lived a life full of adventure that would later be reflected in a collection of stories entitled *Facts, Fiction, Fantasies and Foolishness*. His family helps to keep his memory alive through The Romeo Lemay Contest, which they have generously funded since his passing in 2013. Romeo was an original member of Safety Harbor Writers & Poets and his friendship is remembered fondly.

**Stephen Lindow** took an MFA in English from UMass-Amherst in 2004. He toured with Poetry Alive! and taught middle school and college. Published poems include *Massachusetts Review, Bateau, ARTillery*. He was poetry editor for *Naugatuck Review* and slam judge at W. New England College. Lindow is a noisician who performed Kurt Schwitters's "Ursonata" with a Dadaist group. He is also a member of the experimental musical group Electric Arugula. He lives in Florida.

**Shelly Miller** enjoys exploring a variety of techniques and materials in the process of creating visual expressions of life's experiences of mind, body, and soul. For personal artistic inspiration and growth, Shelly has participated in numerous local art league drawing, painting, and mixed-media classes, including drawing workshops in Italy and Guatemala and has facilitated multiple youth community art projects in collaboration with local artists and artisans.

**Jean F. Morciglio, Ph.D.**, is an instructor, author, and facilitator with over 35 years of experience in higher education. Retired, she now teaches Life Story Writing for the Bloomingdale Writers Connection and The Story Circle Network. As the owner of *Flowing Glass Publications*, she believes in the power of narrative to change lives.

**Micki Morency** is Haitian-American and has lived in Florida for the past 35 years. She is a graduate of Northeastern University from Boston, Mass and The Institute for Writers in 2013. She is married and is the mother of two daughters. Her works have been published online and in print, including *The Tampa Bay Times, The Weekly Challenger, The Peoria Star Journal.*

**Peter Moretti** is a queer poet and scientist who was born and raised in Safety Harbor, Florida. His work frequently reflects on his experiences as a transgender man and relationship with gender, nature, and chosen family. Thanks to Babbo and the open mic crew—your love and encouragement helped shape a shy young poet into a (slightly more) confident young man.

Born in Brooklyn, NY, **Bradley Morewood** moved to the Tampa Bay area in 1975 and now lives in Tampa. He began writing poetry as a child, his first poem being about his hero at the time, John Glenn, the first American to orbit Earth. He explores many subjects in his poetry but is fascinated in particular with psychology.

**Kaitlin Murphy-Knudsen** is an editor and writer in Safety Harbor, and her publication history includes *Newsweek, The Washington Post, Odet, Big Sky Weekly, The Barrington Times*, blogs for educational foundations, and other publications. She has taught writing at American University, SUNY Buffalo, Union County College, and the University of Tampa. In 2018 her poem "Fountain of Youth: St. Augustine, FL" won honorable mention in *Peauxdunque Review's* Words & Music Writing Competition and will be published in the fall. Her short story "Heat" was 2nd place winner of the Romeo Lemay Writing Contest, and her essay "Hail Mary, Full of Grace (for Margaret)" received an honorable mention in the Writer's Digest Awards.

**Rhonda J. Nelson**'s published work includes *Musical Chair* (Ashinga Press, 2004), *The Undertow* (Rattapallax Press, 2001), and individual poems in many journals. She is a Florida Fellow in Poetry (2000-2001), winner of Writer's Exchange 2000, sponsored by *Poets & Writers, Inc.* and recipient of two Hillsborough County Emerging Artist grants and one Hillsborough County Individual Artist grant. She placed first in *Creative Loafing*'s 2018 Best of the Bay for Spoken Word.

**Lee Ellen Noto** resides in St. Petersburg. She taught high school and community college in the Tampa Bay area, Sacramento, and elsewhere. Traveling to Central America and serving as a Peace Corps volunteer, a Big Sister, and a camp counselor in Chicago, has made her sensitive to others. She earned her Ph.D. from USF. She enjoys writing poetry and prose.

**Brooks Nuzum** is a native Floridian who lives in Lake County. He is thirteen and in 8th grade. Brooks is constantly reading and writing plays and musicals, and when he's not writing them, he's performing in them. He loves the old pioneer spirit of Civil War-era Florida and enjoys weaving those elements into his writing.

**Robin O'Dell** is a full-time Florida resident. She is a book lover and insatiable reader. She's been an editor since 2007, working on everything from academic tomes from Harvard University Press to steamy romances from Harlequin. She has edited bestselling and award-winning authors' work, and has helped streamline and tighten first-time authors' prose.

**Patrick Patterson** was always fascinated by photography while growing up. Out of his desire to improve his nature photography and dabble in astrophotography he picked up his first DSLR in 2013. He now enjoys shooting sports, nature, stars, and everything in between.

**Anda Peterson** has lived in St. Pete, Florida full-time for the past thirteen years. She teaches professional and creative writing as an adjunct at the University of South Florida, St. Petersburg.

**Cathy Rebhun** has had short pieces published by *Reader's Digest*, the Florida Writer's Association, *Odet*, and *Parade* magazine. She belongs to a writing critique group and lives in Hillsborough County, Florida, with her husband and two enthusiastic golden retrievers.

Now living in Vero Beach, Florida, **Barry Shapiro** has enjoyed a long career in art, advertising and film. After graduation from Pratt Institute he traveled extensively before settling in Manhattan where he developed a personal style of painting while also working as an apprentice art restorer. Several years later he worked as an illustrator/designer and later became an award winning TV producer/director. He is the co-author of an historic screenplay about the artist Suzanne Valadon.

Raised on a steady diet of words and art, **Jennifer Stott** is one-third of a triplet set. She grew up in suburbia and found escape through reading and writing. Now a full-time college student at USF St. Petersburg, Jennifer currently writes novels she hopes to one day publish.

**Linda Sullivan** retired after teaching middle school for over three decades. She has won twenty-six prizes in local writing contests and recently self-published *Short Stuff*, a young adult novel. Currently, she volunteers at her church, a kindergarten class, and participates in a weekly creative writing group. In addition, she enjoys spending time with family and friends.

**Jonathan Tennis** is a graduate of Eckerd College (BA), Norwich University (MSIA) and the University of Tampa (MFA). He resides in Tampa, Florida where he enjoys writing, reading, year-round sunshine, traveling, and cycling with his partner. His work has appeared in the *Eckerd Review, Military Experience and the Arts, O-Dark-Thirty, Odet, Proud to Be: Writing by American Warriors, Sanctuary Literary and Arts Journal*, and a Festschrift in honor of the poet Peter Meinke.

**Fairl Thomas** is a junior at Eckerd College majoring in Environmental Studies/Animal Studies and minoring in Biology. Fairl volunteers with Wright Ranch Wildlife Rescue and Birds in Helping Hands and is currently conducting Brown Pelican Research for Audubon Society. She enjoys wildlife photography as a hobby.

**Terrie Dahl Thomas** is originally from Pennsylvania but has lived in Safety Harbor for 35 years. She graduated from Edinboro University of PA with a degree in Environmental Studies/Geography and minoring in Geology. Terrie does Gyotaku art and photography, and her photography is currently on display with Safety Harbor Artwalk and is located in Gregario's Restaurant, also in the Rigsby Center and on the cover of the book *A Brief History of Safety Harbor, Florida*. Terrie volunteers for Wildlife Haven and Birds in Helping Hands. Terrie is married to Chip Thomas, a life-long Safety Harbor resident and has a daughter who attends Eckerd College.

**Cheryl A. Van Beek** is grateful to have won first place for Poetry in Odet's 2018 Romeo Lemay Contest and to have had poems published with *Odet, River Poets Journal, Sandhill Review, Poeming Pigeon* and many other publications. Besides the transformative power of writing in different forms, she is passionate about nature, food, art and travel. Living with her wonderful husband and their two cats in Wesley Chapel, she draws great inspiration from Florida's unique beauty.

**Alaina Virgilio** is a 30-year-old freelance photographer from Tampa Bay, Florida. Inspired by the world around her, she tries to capture images that evoke emotion. Self-taught and constantly curious, she finds art in everything.

**Janet Watson** has lived in Pasco County (Wesley Chapel) for over 35 years. She has been a writer and an editor for several local newspapers and is the current president of New River Poets, a chapter of Florida State Poets Association. Poetry has been her literary genre of choice for a long time, and she has published a collection of her poems entitled *Eyes Open, Listening*, but she enjoys writing in many forms. Her most recent project is a novel for middle-grade readers.

CPSIA information can be obtained
at www.ICGtesting.com
Printed in the USA
FSHW011813120820

9 781942 679127